Acclaim for *The Cabin*

A breathtaking journey back and forth through time, through dream-space, and through magical realms. A celebration of the power of love and reverence for life that knows no limits or bounds.

–Donna Henes, author of *The Queen of My Self*

Full of Byzantine twists and turns, Smoky Trudeau's *The Cabin* is a fascinating read. This truly beautiful tale of humanity's connection to the natural realm and to a force we cannot see teaches us that the world is, indeed, a wondrous place full of magic we do not understand. I highly recommend this haunting tale.

–Vila SpiderHawk, author of *Hidden Passages: Tales to Honor the Crones* and *Forest Song: Finding Home*

The Cabin

by

Smoky Trudeau

Vanilla Heart Publishing

USA

The Cabin

Copyright 2008 Smoky Trudeau

Published by:
Vanilla Heart Publishing
www.vanillaheartbookssandauthors.com
10121 Evergreen Way, 25-156
Everett, WA 98204 USA

This book is a work of fiction. Names, characters, places, and incidents are either the product of the author's imagination or are used fictitiously, and any resemblance to places, events, or persons living or dead is purely coincidental.

ISBN: 978-0-9814739-5-6
Library of Congress Control Number 2008922110

10 9 8 7 6 5 4 3 2 1 First Edition

First Printing, March 2008
Printed in the United States of America

Cover Design: Kimberlee Williams

Dedication

To my friends who are my sisters: Kat Anderson, Melinda McIntosh, Susan Gesslein, and the women of GoddessCreative; and to my sisters who are my friends: Bonnie Houff and Mary Ann Shields. You women rock!

Chapter 1

1846

There was a deep connectedness between mountain women in the Allegheny Mountains of Virginia, a connectedness that transcended the tangible, yet was as real as the forest itself. It was a part of the mountain magic her grandmother had taught her when she was a young child, and it was particularly strong between Corrine and her sister, Catherine.

For this reason alone, Corrine never doubted her sister would know when it was time to come; would know when her baby was about to make her entrance into the world. Whatever distance lay between them, with Corrine living in the cabin on Hoffmann Mountain and Catherine in the valley below, one always knew when she was needed by the other. Just as Corrine, gifted in the healing properties of herbs, had arrived on Catherine's doorstep with willow bark tea and a soothing slippery elm elixir hours after Catherine had taken to her bed with fever and cough, Catherine, blessed with a midwife's knowledge and skill, had swept into the cabin as the first pains of labor gripped Corrine's belly.

The childbirth had been difficult, far more difficult than what she'd experienced when her son was born three years prior. But Catherine had remained calm, her voice soothing, encouraging Corrine through every contraction while William, Corrine's husband, fretted a trail of footprints from the bedroom door to the hearth and back again as he tried to console Cyrus, who, bewildered by his mother's screams of pain, wailed with equal intensity.

"I'm going to die," Corrine whispered to her sister. "I saw it in a dream. William, and Cyrus, and the baby, but I was gone." She let out a gasp as yet another contraction wracked her body. Catherine took her sister's feet in her hands, pressing firmly on the soft pad of her heel and the inside corner of her ankle until the pain eased and the contraction passed.

"You aren't going to die. I'm not going to let you die." Catherine dipped a rag into a pitcher of water, and mopped the sweat from Corrine's face and chest.

"Promise me…Catherine, look at me!"

Catherine put down the rag.

"Promise me, if anything happens to me…" One last contraction and with a bloodcurdling scream, she pushed her daughter into the world.

Corrine could hear the forest calling her, whispering her name as the soft winds of spring warmed the mountain.

She'd never gone so many days without walking through her beloved forest, along its streams and game trails. Since Elizabeth's birth, she had been too tired and weak to do more than walk to the creek and back. But with Catherine insisting on staying on to help out with the children, she had finally regained her strength and at last was free to escape the stifling confines of the cabin and roam the mountainside once again.

True, it made her husband nervous when she went off by herself. She wasn't sure why—William was a circuit rider preacher, and often was gone for months at a time as he rode the circuit, preaching the gospel at every home and village in the Shenandoah Valley that would have him. Perhaps when he was gone he simply imagined she stayed tucked cozily into the mountainside cabin, never venturing beyond the gardens, small pasture and barn. And while she didn't wish to cause him anxiety with her forays away from the safety of the cabin, he really did worry needlessly. She felt as at home walking through the woods as a bear or bobcat might. Corrine was raised in the mountains. Mountain women were both strong and intuitive. She was confident William knew in his head she was capable of fending for herself and their two children, but she recognized his heart often told him something different.

Today she was headed for the mountain's lower elevations. The family was running low on slippery elm, and with both a toddler and a baby in the house, Corrine didn't want to run out of the magical bark that eased everything from sore throats and teething pain to scraped knees and constipation. It was also mushroom season, and with any luck she'd come home with a bucket of morels to fry up for supper.

She'd have to walk and work fast. Elizabeth was small, but she had a voracious appetite. Corrine had, at best, three hours before her breasts would fill, sensing her daughter's hunger even before the tiny girl cried out. She felt sorry for Catherine if she wasn't back in time to appease the baby's squalls.

After kissing her children good-bye and thanking Catherine at least a dozen times, Corrine grabbed a pail and a basket and danced out the front door of the cabin and into the forest.

The first thing she noticed was the smell. It was the same scent she had breathed in every time she walked in forest, but this time, she could break down the individual essences perfuming the air: rotting rhododendron blossoms mixed with moss-covered granite and cold, crisp water. She had never noticed granite had a scent—like the air during a thunderstorm, right after lightning struck—or that water could smell cold. The discovery delighted her.

Corrine instinctively knew where to turn off the trail to find the slippery elm grove, for she had been harvesting bark from these same trees for years. She said a quick prayer of thanks to the trees before taking the sharp knife she had packed in her basket and starting to work.

She quickly peeled the tough outer bark from several branches, then peeled the tender inner layer of bark, cutting the strips into pieces small enough to fit in the basket. She was careful to select only a few branches from each tree before moving on to another. William laughed at her belief that trees had spirits, but she knew better. Her grandmother had been part Cherokee Indian, and had taught Corrine that everything in nature had a spirit. To dishonor these spirits by taking too many limbs from a tree or girdling its trunk was unthinkable.

She found the first morels under the second tree, growing along the south-facing slope. Using a firm but gentle hand, she sliced the mushrooms about an inch above the ground.

Mushrooms are interesting, she thought. Cut a tree or a shrub down to the ground and it might or might not grow back. Morels, on the other hand, always sprang back up, even when you harvested every one you found.

She worked for thirty minutes, peeling slippery elm bark and harvesting mushrooms. She left half the morels she found for the bears, skunks, and raccoons that called Hoffmann Mountain home, for she knew they favored mushrooms, especially in the early spring before the berries ripened.

The last mushroom cap hid a treasure unlike any Corrine had ever seen. It was a small stone, about the size of a chestnut, in the perfect shape of a cross. She tried to pick it up, but something was rooting it firmly in the ground. Using her knife as a spade, she carefully excavated the stone from its place. At last, it broke free.

To her surprise, the stone was not one cross but three, each one perfectly formed, each anchored firmly in the smooth, rounded stone she now held in her hand. They looked like they had simply grown out of the stone, like corn sprouting from the ground.

She carried the stone to the stream to wash away the dirt still clinging to it. She knelt on a smooth, flat boulder and plunged the stone into the creek. The water was cold, and her fingers soon grew numb, but Corrine barely noticed, so intent was she on cleaning the stone. At last, satisfied she'd removed every last trace of dirt, she lifted the stone from the water and clamored to her feet.

Wet and clean, the rock was slippery, and before she realized what was happening, it slipped from her numb fingers and crashed to the rock on which she stood. The stone broke neatly in two.

Corrine picked up the pieces. She was thankful to see the crosses themselves hadn't been damaged. Two of them were still firmly attached to the rock. The third cross, however, had been neatly severed from its base.

The solitary cross felt surprisingly warm in her hand, not cool as she would have expected. What a wonderful gift to take William, she thought.

But only the one, solitary cross. Her grandmother had taught her that not only the plants and animals but also the stones and the Earth itself had spirits. She would leave the two crosses still clinging to the stone here in the forest.

She looked around for a suitable place to put them; a place where animals and wind and rain wouldn't disturb them. She decided on a mossy crevice in a large granite boulder midway between the creek and the path that led back up to the cabin.

Satisfied the crosses were in a safe place, she pocketed the solitary cross, then retrieved her basket and headed back up the mountain. Her breasts were starting to tingle, and she tried hard not to think about her daughter, knowing the consequence of such thoughts. But it was no use trying not to think of her precious baby, and a moment later the front of her dress darkened as her milk flowed.

Cyrus was waiting for her on the stone steps leading to the cabin's front door. "Mamma, Mamma!" he screamed when he saw her. He ran across the clearing as quickly as his short legs would carry him. Corrine dropped the basket to the ground and gathered her son in her arms.

"Were you a good boy for your Aunt Catherine?" she asked, carrying him back to the cabin.

The little boy nodded his head. " 'Listbeth pooped.'" He turned up his nose in disgust.

Corrine smiled. "Elizabeth does that a lot, doesn't she?" She pushed open the cabin door and carried Cyrus inside. "Catherine, William, I'm back," she called.

"We're out here," her sister answered from behind the house. "I've made tea."

Corrine took a few steps toward the back door, then remembered the basket she'd set down out front. "You wait here, Cyrus," she said, setting him down and turning back to retrieve her basket. "Mamma will be right back."

Despite his father's gentle cajoling, then firm insistence that Cyrus tell the truth; despite the promise of licorice, then threat of being sent to bed without any supper if he didn't say what really happened to his mother, Cyrus did not waver from the story he told William and Catherine when they came inside, looking for Corrine: His mother had stepped out the front door and simply disappeared.

Corrine awakened to find herself lying on her side in the grass and staring at a sea of pink blossoms cascading down the slope away from the house. That's odd, she thought, I don't remember the roses being in bloom. Her head hurt, and when she rubbed the sore spot discovered a lump the size of a walnut near her right temple.

"I'm okay, Cyrus," she called. "Mamma just tripped and fell." She stood, shaky and unsteady after her fall. Where was Cyrus? She'd just set him down when she tripped on her way out the door. He must have seen her fall. Why hadn't Catherine or William come to her assistance? Surely she had screamed when she fell...or hadn't she? She couldn't remember.

"Catherine? William?" she called, taking a few unsteady steps toward the cabin. She winced in pain. Her left ankle was badly bruised.

The sight of the cabin caused her to stop dead in her tracks. The stone steps leading to her front door were moss-covered and crumbling. One windowpane was broken; the rest were clouded with dirt and covered in spider webs. The place looked like it had been abandoned for years.

"William?" she called again, fear choking her voice. She hobbled around to the back, where her husband and sister had sat drinking tea just minutes ago.

No one was there. Gone were the pine rocking chairs William had so lovingly crafted when she was expecting Cyrus, chairs made so he could sit and read to her while she nursed and rocked their child. Blackberry brambles blanketed what should have been the freshly cultivated patch of earth that was her vegetable garden. Her massive black iron kettle was gone. The barn was a crumbled pile of rotting wood.

Forgetting her injured ankle, Corrine flew to the back door and threw it open.

The cabin was empty, save for a thick labyrinth of cobwebs and sprinkling of mouse droppings on the floor.

With one gut-wrenching sob, Corrine sank to her knees. The world grew dark as she collapsed in the back doorway of what had once been her home.

It was dark when she awoke once again, but a glow in the eastern sky told her morning was creeping up the mountain, and that soon it would be light. She shivered. How long had she been asleep? Had she lain unconscious in the doorway all night? And what did she do now?

The cabin was empty; her family was gone. Surely those two events could not have happened in the brief period of time she lay in the front yard, after her fall. She didn't even remember falling. She had set Cyrus down in the cabin, turned to go back in the yard to retrieve her basket, and…nothing. She couldn't remember anything between that moment and the moment she opened her eyes to see the roses blooming.

Slowly, she pulled herself to her feet. Her ankle was horribly swollen, and she winced in pain when she tried to put her weight on it. She had to walk, though. She couldn't stay here. She had to find her family.

She limped around the side of the cabin to the front yard, hoping she'd find her basket of mushrooms and elm bark, but it was gone, too.

She'd have to walk down to the valley. She'd find her family. Perhaps they had gone to Catherine's house. Maybe they'd be back, looking for her. If she stuck to the trail, she'd be all right. She'd find them, or they would find her.

She turned and took one last look at the dilapidated cabin before setting off down the mountain.

Corrine hadn't walked ten feet into the forest before she realized something else was desperately wrong. The trail William worked so hard to keep clear was nowhere to be found. All that remained where the path should have been was a narrow animal trail, the kind deer cut through the forest.

She followed the deer trail. At least it was headed in the right direction. A catbird mewed from overhead, scolding and chattering as she limped down the trail. She smiled at the little gray bird, glad to have some company.

She walked another ten minutes. The forest looked different. The majestic chestnut trees that had towered over her the day before—had it only been the day before?—were gone. In their stead were rotting stumps, looking to Corrine like so many gravestones in a chestnut cemetery. Hemlocks, witch hazel, and tulip trees now dominated the landscape.

Even the creek looked different, she realized. It seemed to have changed its course, cutting slightly to the south at one point where she was certain it once flowed straight east.

After an hour, she could walk no farther. She was terribly hungry, and the pain in her ankle was becoming unbearable. She made her way over to the creek and slipped her throbbing ankle into the icy water. Five minutes later, her foot was blue, but at least the pain had dulled.

Exhausted, Corrine leaned against a mossy rock. She reached in her pocket; the stone cross was still there. Clutching it tightly, she closed her eyes and uttered a quick prayer.

Ten minutes later, the stone fell from her limp hand.

Bright whorls of light flashed through Corrine's mind. Her head hurt terribly, and she was burning up with fever. She was in the forest...why was she sleeping in the forest? It was nighttime, and she could feel the sky ablaze with the light of a thousand stars.

"Corrine, Corrine..."

She was in a dream, that was it. A dream that smelled of damp earth and decayed leaves; a dream where she was sitting by the creek, looking for...looking for what?

"Corrine, Corrine..."

"I'm here, Grandmother."

"Corrine...open your eyes!"

She opened them. Standing before her was her old Indian grandmother, glowing like foxfire. Trembling, she bowed her head to the ancient apparition. "Am I dead, then, too?"

The Grandmother chuckled. "No, my child. You are not dead. But you have stumbled upon the ancient fairy magic, and your life has been forevermore changed."

"William, my children…"

"What has become of them I cannot say," the Grandmother said.

"Cannot, or will not? Do you not know?"

"Alas, it is not within my power to speak of things that have transpired," the Grandmother replied. "I cannot tell you what has happened. This you must learn for yourself. But this I can say to you: Believe what you see."

"But I don't understand, Grandmother! Everything is wrong; everything is changed!" Corrine felt a tear slide down her cheek.

"Everything has changed," the Grandmother agreed. "And changed forevermore. But listen to my words, grandchild of my heart, and remember. What was torn asunder must be reunited; only then will this grave wrong be righted."

"Remember what? Grandmother, you're speaking in riddles, and I don't understand!"

The foxfire began to flicker and fade. "What was torn asunder must be reunited; only then will this grave wrong be righted."

"Grandmother, don't leave me. I don't know what I'm supposed to do. Grandmother!"

"Remember, Corrine. What was torn asunder must be reunited…"

She was gone. Corrine sobbed herself back to sleep.

Chapter 2

When James-Cyrus Hoffmann inherited his grandfather's farm, it wasn't the rambling old house or the prize Angus cattle grazing in its pastures that interested him most; but rather an old, dilapidated cabin, deep in the woods and halfway up the mountain.

As a boy, he had dreamed of the cabin, voices of children and women dead long ago playing and laughing in his dreams. A raven-haired girl, dancing around an enormous cauldron, singing songs as her mother stirred the kettle. A boy, looking very much like himself, doing slingshot practice at a target scratched on the side of a rock. A gentleman, rocking in his chair and reading aloud as his family listened.

As an adult, the dreams had taken on a more somber edge. The children grew up, and the boy who looked like him went off to war, the father off to minister to the wounded. The girl and her mother remained alone in the cabin, staring out the window as if looking for someone to arrive. At times, even the mother was gone, and the girl, now a young woman, was left alone.

Recently, the somber dreams had turned to nightmares. Something was after the woman in the woods, something James-Cyrus could neither see nor hear. She was in grave danger, danger that only James-Cyrus could slay. But he always awakened in a cold sweat before the danger got near enough for him to see.

He did not wish to dream anymore. Yet the cabin kept calling him back, in his sleep.

The trail up Hoffmann Mountain led past the family cemetery, where four generations of James-Cyrus's ancestors were buried. Many of the grave markers were no longer legible, the names worried off by rain and wind and time. Still, James-Cyrus knew the names of every soul resting here.

There was William and his wife, Catherine, along with his great-great-grandfather and namesake, Cyrus James, who, although he lived but ninety miles from the capital of the Confederacy, fought for the north during the Civil War. His wife Rosalee was next to him.

Next came Nathaniel, Cyrus and Rosalee's only son, and his wife Rebekkah. James-Cyrus's grandfather, Samuel, had been their last-born and only surviving child. Eight small white markers bore painful witness to the brothers and sisters who were born before him, only to die within a few months, days, or in three cases, hours of birth.

His parents were buried here: Eliza, who died giving birth to James-Cyrus in an era where few women suffered that fate; and Zachariah, so despondent over his wife's death he put a bullet through his head when his son was but a few hours old.

A mound of freshly turned earth drew James-Cyrus over the crumbling stone walls surrounding the cemetery. He knelt at the grave, at last allowing the tears to flow that had fought for release since his grandfather's death two weeks earlier. He wiped a splatter of fresh soil from the headstone. Samuel James Hoffmann, the stone read.

"I don't mean to disrespect your wishes, Granddaddy, but I'm heading up the mountain this morning. I can't hardly sleep for the nightmares. I need to know what's up there. I hope you understand." He paused, as if waiting for his grandfather to answer him, but the gentle wind breezing through the valley was his only reply.

"Well, then." James-Cyrus rose to his feet, wiping his dirty hands on the back of his khaki hiking shorts. "Good-bye, Granddaddy."

He turned to leave, pausing as something unusual caught his eye. Nestled among the clods of freshly turned earth covering his grandfather was a tiny treasure that both surprised and delighted James-Cyrus.

It was a fairy stone, perfectly formed in the shape of a Maltese cross. He picked it up, turning it over and over in his hand, examining it closely. The stone was large, nearly an inch-and-a-half square. James-Cyrus had dozens of the staurolite crystal crosses in an old canning jar back at the house, souvenirs from a camping trip to Fairy Stone Park he and his grandfather had taken when he was nine years old. None of the stones in his collection were nearly this large, nor this perfectly shaped.

"Fairy stones aren't found in this part of Virginia," he muttered to himself. "Where the heck did this come from?" He gently toed dirt, but found nothing more.

He stuck the stone in his pocket, took one more look at his grandfather's grave, then jumped back over the stone wall and made his way into the forest.

Pausing a few feet into the woods, James-Cyrus waited for his eyes to adjust to the cool darkness. A blue jay shrieked overhead, alerting the forest inhabitants to the presence of the intruder. The high-pitched whine of a mosquito in his right ear was silenced with one swat of his hand.

Which way? Several deer trails converged at the spot James-Cyrus was standing, but none looked exactly as he remembered. It had been twenty years since he first found his way up the mountain to the cabin, and the trail he had discovered as a boy had all but vanished in a tangle of dogwood, rhododendron, and fallen oaks bejeweled in brightly colored fungi.

That rock. He'd gone around that big rock. Confident that he was on the right track, James-Cyrus forged ahead, ignoring the sharp thorns of the blackberry canes menacing his bare legs.

The mixture of guilt and excitement that had carried him as a boy of ten up the mountain returned, urging him on. As a child, he was forbidden to hike the trail behind the cemetery. About that his grandfather had been adamant.

"There's things up in those woods you don't understand, boy," he told James-Cyrus. "Leave them be."

His grandfather's refusal to discuss the trail and what lay at its far end had made James-Cyrus all the more curious about what was in the woods. Early one morning, when he was supposed to be gathering eggs in the henhouse, he slipped into the woods behind the cemetery, praying his grandfather hadn't seen him.

He almost made it. The cabin had just come into view when he felt a firm grip on his shoulders, spinning him around so fast he tripped, stumbling right into his grandfather.

"Didn't I tell you never to come up this mountain, boy?" his grandfather said in a coarse whisper. "Go back to the house this instant!"

"But Granddaddy, there's a cabin up here! It looks just like the cabin in my dreams! What's—"

"I said go back home! Please, James-Cyrus, just do it!"

"Aren't you coming?" James-Cyrus had suddenly been afraid. "Aren't you coming too, Granddaddy?"

"I'll be along in a minute. Just go...now!"

James-Cyrus ran.

He knew better than to talk about what happened when his grandfather returned later that night. Neither one of them spoke of the incident again. James-Cyrus spent the rest of his youth trying to forget what he had seen on the mountainside.

His dreams would not allow him to forget.

The path became a little clearer half a mile up the mountain, kept open by deer and bear, James-Cyrus suspected. The climb was steep and rugged, and he tried to pace himself so as not to tire. Adrenaline pushed him onward, and he stopped only once, when he came to a rushing stream he remembered from his childhood foray up the mountain.

He splashed the icy water over his face and back of his neck, sending a shiver down his spine. A ground squirrel ran out on a rotting log dangling over the stream. Twitching his tail furiously, the squirrel scolded James-Cyrus soundly for invading his territory.

"Take it easy, little man. I just need to catch my breath and have a bite to eat." He pulled a bag of trail mix from his daypack and tossed a handful of raw cashews and dried cherries to the squirrel. "Here, you want some?"

The squirrel stuffed the nuts and fruit into his cheeks, then gave James-Cyrus one last glare before disappearing into his hole.

James-Cyrus sat on a rock, eating trail mix and examining the fairy stone he'd found. It had rained the previous evening; that must be what churned it up, he surmised. He'd been out to the gravesite every day since his grandfather's funeral. He would have noticed it if it had been there before.

Fairy stones had, at one time, been fairly common over in Patrick County, where Fairy Stone Park was located. But that was more than one hundred miles from where this stone had been found. To James-Cyrus's knowledge, fairy stones had never been found in this part of Virginia.

It was their friend and neighbor and James-Cyrus's surrogate aunt, Cora Spellmacher, who had first told him the legend of the fairy stone when he was a child. Cora had been making apple butter, and James-Cyrus was helping out, keeping the wood fire stoked beneath the black cast iron kettle bubbling with the tantalizing brew of apples and cinnamon and cloves.

"Many, many years before Chief Powhatan and his people roamed the woods and valleys of Virginia, the fairies made this their home." Cora stirred as she talked, her golden eyes staring into the kettle as if they and not the fire beneath were what caused it to stew. "The fairies led a carefree, happy life, dancing around a beautiful spring and playing with the elves. But one day, their happy existence came to an end. An elfin messenger came from a land far away to tell the fairies of the death of Jesus Christ. The fairies wept with sorrow, their tears crystallizing into beautiful crosses as they fell to earth. Not long after that, the fairies themselves disappeared."

"Aw, Cora, that ain't true." James-Cyrus, at eight, thought himself too mature to believe in fairies and elves. "You don't really believe that."

Cora put down her spoon and pulled the little boy into her ample arms. She smelled of cinnamon and rose water. "There's more to this world than what you see with your two eyes, James-Cyrus. Do you believe the pharaohs of ancient Egypt really existed?"

"Well of course—Granddaddy took me to the Smithsonian last summer, and we saw mummies and a movie about the pyramids and all sorts of stuff from ancient Egypt."

Cora released him and resumed her stirring. "You know the pharaohs lived because they left proof. Well, what's a fairy stone if not proof the fairies really lived?"

James-Cyrus hadn't known what to say to Cora about that. But that night, he'd had a dream, a dream he still remembered as vividly as if he had dreamt it last night.

He was among the fairies, living happily in the mountains, dancing and singing and playing, when suddenly a raven appeared in the sky. The fairies huddled together, hushed, as the raven spoke.

"The one known as the Christ has been murdered," the raven said, "hung on a cross by those of his own kind."

The fairies held each other and sobbed, and as each tear hit the ground, it formed the shape of a cross. But one fairy's grief was so deep she took wing, flying over mountain and valley, flying blind, until she was hopelessly lost. When exhaustion overcame her, she collapsed in a grove of trees, shed three last perfect tears, and died.

After that dream, James-Cyrus had insisted his grandfather take him to Fairy Stone Park to search himself for evidence fairies once lived there. The jar of fairy stones sitting on his dresser back at the house was all the proof he'd needed as a young boy.

He put the stone back in his pocket and continued up the trail.

He was on the verge of giving up and turning back when the cabin came into view, standing in the middle of a clearing. It was small compared to his old Victorian house in the valley below, but would probably have been considered large and quite nice in its day, he guessed. The stone steps leading to the front door were crumbling, and the old-fashioned roses growing beside it had run amok, cascading down the hillside like a pink waterfall. A large hemlock tree stood sentry on the far side, casting a protective shadow over the cabin.

He picked his way carefully up the stairs. The last thing he needed was to slip on a crumbling bit of stone and break an ankle. The thought briefly alarmed him, and he chided himself for not telling Cora where he was going. He knew better than to strike off alone into the woods without someone knowing where he was and when he would return. But it was too late to do that now.

He grabbed the door handle and pushed. The door was warped with age, and it took several hard shoves before it gave way and swung open. He stepped into the dim room.

"Brother! You're home!" The woman threw herself into his arms.

"Hey, hold on there!" James-Cyrus struggled to free himself from the woman's embrace. "You've made a mistake. I'm not your brother, and I don't have a sister. Who are you? What are you doing here?"

The woman stepped back, laughing. "It's me, Cyrus. It's Elizabeth." She grabbed the sides of her long skirt and twirled around. "I know I've grown up. I turned twenty last week, after all. But have I changed that much in a year's time, brother?"

"I already told you, I'm not your brother." Confusion washed over him like a fever. The woman looked vaguely familiar, but he certainly wasn't her brother. And she certainly did not belong here. "What are you doing on my property? It's dangerous to be up here all alone."

"Your property? You mean our property, Cyrus." She looked as puzzled as he felt. "Papa's property."

She stepped closer, taking his arm gently in her hand and examining his face closely. "Are you well, Cyrus? You aren't wounded? You seem...confused."

"I'm confused? Miss, it seems to me you're the one who's confused." He reached up to push her arm away, but froze, hand mid-air.

His arm was swathed in navy wool, not the green cotton plaid of the shirt he'd been wearing. Cold sweat beaded on his forehead as he looked down at the four-button navy coat and light blue trousers he was now wearing. Worn, dusty black leather shoes were where his hiking boots had been just minutes earlier. He reached up and pulled his hat from his head. Briefly comforted by the feel of the brim, his heart sank when what was supposed to be his favorite Baltimore Orioles baseball cap turned out to be a leather-billed forage cap the same navy blue color of his coat.

James-Cyrus's legs began to shake uncontrollably. Bile rose in his throat. He recognized the clothing he was wearing.

"What the hell am I doing in a Union soldier's uniform?" he whispered.

"Cyrus, you're not well!" Elizabeth grabbed him as his knees buckled and eased him into a chair. "Let me fetch some water for you." She stepped out the back door of the cabin and reappeared moments later with a dipper of water.

He took the dipper and drank deeply. "Thank you," he whispered hoarsely. "I'm...I'm not myself." He finished the water and handed the dipper back to Elizabeth. "More. Please."

He looked wildly around the cabin. It was furnished plainly, with a table and four chairs. Two caned rocking chairs set before the fireplace. He could see a large bed in the adjoining room, and a chest of drawers exactly like the one in his grandfather's old bedroom at home. A ladder led to an overhead loft.

Elizabeth returned with a pail of water. Greedily, James-Cyrus downed another two dippers full. His gut reacted like he had been punched, doubling him over in pain.

"I'm going to be sick," he whispered. He staggered out of his chair and through the front door, stumbling down the stairs before collapsing on the ground, vomiting.

Stomach empty, he rolled over on his back, staring at the sky. The afternoon sun was warm on his bare legs; the scratches from the blackberry brambles were beginning to sting.

Bare legs. James-Cyrus struggled to sit up, staring at his scratched legs. Gone were the heavy wool trousers and jacket; he was wearing his own clothes again.

He was back. But where had he been?

Chapter 3

Cora lugged the final basket of wool from the shearing shed to the large cauldrons of water heating over an open fire in the middle of her back yard. Samuel and James-Cyrus had helped with the shearing late in March, as they always did. Even though the Hoffmanns raised cattle, not sheep, they'd become expert shearers over the years, and rare was the fleece that did not come off the sheep in one piece. They had helped her skirt the fleece, too, a process that always somewhat irritated Cora. Cutting away the top few inches of wool seemed like such a waste, but it inevitably was too dirty, matted, and burr-encrusted to be of any use.

The sheep had been unusually cooperative this year, a fact she attributed to the dried chamomile and valerian root she'd liberally sprinkled in the sheep's watering trough every day for a week before the shearing. If the herbs helped people relax, Cora reasoned, there was no reason they couldn't calm her sheep as well. Samuel and James-Cyrus had laughed when she told them her plan, but their laughter had turned to, well, sheepishness when they came to help with the shearing and saw how cooperative the normally ornery animals had become. Cora knew her herbs, knew the magic they possessed. She'd never had a doubt—she was just upset with herself for not having thought of it years earlier.

She set down the basket of fleece and stuck her hand in the first cauldron, testing the water temperature. It was perfect. She grabbed the pitchfork leaning against the back steps and used it to knock some of the burning logs out from beneath the kettle, so the water wouldn't continue to heat, then stirred in the homemade lye soap that would coax the grease from the fleece.

"You look like Lady MacBeth. Bubble bubble, toil and trouble, or whatever it was she said."

Cora looked up to see James-Cyrus striding across the back yard, grinning from ear to ear.

"Your Shakespeare's a bit rusty, love." She checked the water in the second cauldron. It was still too cool. "The witches said that, not Lady MacBeth. Who was out of her mind crazy, by the way, which I am not."

"If anyone else saw you standing there, stirring a cauldron and your hair sticking out all over the place like that, they'd disagree." He gave Cora a quick peck on the cheek.

"It's the humidity. Makes my hair a little wild. Just because I'm sixty years old doesn't mean I have to go get one of those old lady cuts everyone else wears. I haven't cut my hair in twenty years; I don't intend to start now." She pulled the rubber band from her silver-gray hair, smoothed it back as best she could, then re-banded it. "There. Do I look less witchy now?"

"Absolutely gorgeous."

Cora pulled a fleece from the basket and carefully dipped it in the cauldron, being careful not to swish it through the water, which would have resulted in twisted, ruined fibers.

James-Cyrus collapsed to the ground and lay on his back, hands behind his head. He was too close to the cauldron, and Cora gave his feet a kick to encourage him to move.

"Why do you always insist on processing your own wool?" he said, pulling up his knees. "It's so time consuming for you. I'd think you'd do better to send it to a mill or something."

"Technology is of little use in some things, James-Cyrus." She tested the second cauldron again; it was warming up nicely. "Processing and spinning wool is an ancient, sacred art. There's nothing sacred in a machine doing my wool."

He grinned. "Everything is sacred to you."

She didn't reply, instead sinking none-too-gracefully into a heap on the grass next to James-Cyrus. Her bones were tingling. Not really aching, like when her arthritis flared up. Just tingling. Something was up with James-Cyrus. Her bones were never wrong.

"Cora, did you ever go up the mountain with Granddaddy? Do you know what's up there?" He picked a pebble from the grass and tossed it at the kettle.

Cora stared into the glowing embers beneath the kettles. "I'm not one for guessing games. Why don't you just tell me."

She listened intently as James-Cyrus poured out the story of his encounter with the young woman in the cabin on the mountainside, acutely aware of the similarities between his story and his grandfather's before him, noting with interest the differences. Samuel had been terrified by the strange things that happened when he stumbled upon the cabin, and he had been adamant about James-Cyrus not knowing about the place. Cora had respected his wishes while he was alive, but Samuel was gone now, and James-Cyrus had discovered the cabin on his own.

"...and the next thing I know, I'm lying outside in the grass, puking my guts out. But at least I'm me again."

"What you're wanting to know is if what you experienced yesterday was real or if you imagined the entire thing, am I correct?" She stood; it was time to rinse the fleece.

"I had to be imagining it, didn't I?" He didn't sound certain.

Using a bucket, Cora dipped warm water out of the second kettle and poured it into a rinsing trough. The fleece would need to be rinsed at least three or four times; she always used a separate trough for rinsing so as not to foul all the rinse water at once. She pulled the fleece from the water and held it high above the cauldron, allowing the soapy water to drain out. She didn't speak as she worked, but rather concentrated on breathing deeply and steadily, and trying to slow her racing heart.

"Make yourself useful here and drain this trough," she instructed him after she'd dipped the soapy fleece into the rinse a time or two. "Then refill it with fresh water."

He rose and did as he was told. "Are you going to answer my question, Cora? Do you think what I saw was real?"

She went back to dipping the fleece. Once more she asked him to drain and refill the rinsing trough, once more he did as he was told. When at last the fleece was rinsed clean of all grease and soap, she carried it around the house to the front porch, and gently arranged it on the drying rack she had set up earlier. James-Cyrus followed close at her heels. Just like a puppy, she thought with some amusement.

"Tea?" She asked, waving him in the direction of the old caned rocking chairs on the porch.

"Sure," he said, plopping down in one of the chairs, "if you'll then tell me what you think happened to me."

"Patience, my boy, patience." She went inside just long enough to get a pitcher of iced tea from the refrigerator and two glasses, along with a jar of rosehip jam and some freshly baked graham crackers. She carried the tray of refreshments to the porch and set it on the wicker table between the rockers.

"The universe is a magical and mystical place, James-Cyrus," she said as she poured tea. "People who think everything can be explained by scientific theory or reasoning end up stumbling through life, not seeing many of the wonders that are right before their eyes if they'd only take time to look." She took the cracker and jam he handed her. "Thanks. I do make good crackers and jam, don't I? So much better than what you buy at the store."

"Everything you make is wonderful, Cora," he agreed, taking a huge bite from his cracker. "You're the only one I've ever heard of who bakes her own graham crackers."

"Don't talk with your mouth full. But thanks. Tell me, have you ever driven down the highway and seen a heron or egret or deer, and pulled over to watch it for a while?"

"Sure," he said, taking another cracker. "I do that anytime I see wildlife. It always amazes me that all the other cars just keep on whizzing by, like they don't see what I—" He stopped before he finished his sentence. "That's what you mean, isn't it Cora. People don't take the time to look."

"That's exactly what I mean. That heron or egret or deer is invisible to all those other drivers, because they don't look for it. They don't see. Now, what does this have to do with what happened to you yesterday?"

"I don't know."

He sounded frustrated, but Cora knew that in order for him to believe the magic was real, he'd have to figure what had happened by himself.

"Think it through. Don't reject in your head what you know to be true in your heart just because it doesn't sound plausible to your rational self. Sometimes our rational selves are wrong."

"My head is telling me that I could not possibly have stepped back in time by about a hundred and forty years when I walked through that cabin door. My heart is telling me that is exactly what I did."

Setting down his tea glass, he jumped to his feet. "I'm going back. I have to go back, and try to figure this thing out. I have to figure out why Granddaddy didn't want me up there, why he was afraid." He hit the stairs at a run, not looking back at her. "I'll see you later, Cora. I love you!"

She watched him jump in his battered old Ford truck and tear off down the lane before getting up herself. She took the snack tray to the kitchen, rinsed the dishes, then made her way back to the yard, where the cauldron fires were dying. She stared into the water of the ancient one.

The reflection of a young, raven-haired beauty stared back.

Elizabeth Hoffmann took down a basket hanging from the ceiling beams and slowly made her way out the back door to the garden. Her mother had been gone for two days, midwifing a woman who lived in the valley below. Elizabeth promised her the sugar snap peas would be picked and ready for canning by the time she returned. But sometimes Mamma was gone several days when she midwifed, so Elizabeth had decided to start the canning herself.

She was alone when Mamma left—Papa had been riding the circuit for the past six months, ministering to Yankee and Rebel soldier alike—but she didn't mind being left alone up on the mountain. In fact, she cherished the solitude. She felt herself to be as much a part of the mountain as the brook that bubbled near the clearing, or the bear or deer or possum that called the mountain home. She'd never been afraid to be alone. That is, until yesterday.

Cyrus had not returned after bolting from the house. She'd tried to follow him, but it was as if he had vanished into thin air. She'd circled the cabin, and called to him, but her only reply was the sweet song of a scarlet tanager perched in the hemlock at the edge of the clearing.

She stoked the fire beneath the large outdoor cauldron used to boil water for canning. Satisfied the water was heating properly, she headed for the garden, setting her basket on the ground before gently twisting pea pods from the vine.

Cyrus hadn't looked injured—no visible wounds, no blood stains on his uniform. He'd walked in as though he'd just returned from a day of deer hunting, not a year of fighting rebel soldiers, yet he hadn't seemed to know where he was, or who she was. What was it he had said? He wasn't himself.

She picked up the basket of peas and moved to the next row. The pea crop had been good this year, and she knew it would take all day today and most of tomorrow to can them all. She didn't mind. She enjoyed canning, and this high up the mountain the air was cool enough that she didn't mind being around the big kettles of boiling water.

Maybe she'd dreamed the entire thing. Maybe Cyrus hadn't returned from the war; maybe she had yearned so long for his return that she had a vision of what was to come. That had happened to her before; dreaming about something only to find it come true a day, a week, a month later. Just last week she'd dreamed about a mother bear with three cubs, and two days later, at twilight, a bear with three young wandered into the clearing and raided their blackberry bushes.

She dusted off her skirt, picked up the basket, and headed back toward the cabin. That must have been what had happened. She'd dreamed the whole thing. A pang of disappointment pierced her breast, but disappointment quickly turned to anticipation. If it was one of her dreams, or visions, or whatever it was she experienced, that meant Cyrus would soon be safely returned to them.

Her joyful anticipation was short-lived as a shiver of dread raced down her spine, and the warm summer morning suddenly felt cold as January. What if her vision meant something more sinister? Maybe someone had discovered Cyrus was fighting for the Yankees and not against them. All Mamma or Papa ever told anyone was that Cyrus had joined the army. They let people draw their own conclusions about which army he'd joined. What if Cyrus had been found out and was now in danger? What if they all were in danger?

She wished her mother was home. Mamma would know what to do. But then, she'd never told her parents about her premonitions, afraid they'd think she'd gone mad. Mamma would probably tell her it was just a wistful dream, and to forget about it. Even if it wasn't a dream, there were times when she thought something was going to happen only to be disappointed when the anticipated event never materialized. It was probably better to keep her experience of the previous day to herself, at least for the time being.

She stopped to check the progress of the heating water, setting the basket of peas on the ground before leaning over the cauldron to test the temperature of the water. What she saw in the warming water took her so by surprise she jumped back, tripping over her skirts and falling over the basket of peas, spilling them onto the ground.

"What is going on here? What's happening to me?" she whispered to the wind as she picked herself up from the ground and cautiously peered into the cauldron once again.

The reflection in the water was not her own.

Chapter 4

By the time James-Cyrus was to the end of Cora's driveway, he realized it was already too late in the day to begin a hike up the mountain. While it stayed light well into the evening down in the valley, the mountain was a different story. The forest was on the dark side at high noon; by the time the sun began slipping toward its bed on the western horizon, it became nearly impossible to see anything beneath the sheltering trees. His return to the cabin would have to wait until morning.

The fairy stone was sitting on the coffee table in his living room at home. Damn. He'd meant to take it to show Cora. Maybe she'd have a theory where it came from.

He picked it up, noticing how comfortably it fit in the palm of his hand. While it was large for a fairy stone, it wasn't a large rock. The edges were smooth and cold, but the center of the cross seemed to warm his palm ever so slightly. Cora would probably tell him it was generating some sort of healing energy. The thought amused him. James-Cyrus adored Cora, but her belief in the mysterious and magical powers hidden in plants and crystals sometimes tried his patience. Although, now that he thought about it, the sheep that spring had been mighty mellow after drinking the water Cora laced with chamomile and valerian. Still, lots of medicines came from plants. His grandfather had taken digitalis for his heart before he died; didn't he read somewhere that came from foxglove? And Cora's syrup made from boiled black cherry bark considerably eased his cough when he'd been so sick with bronchitis the year before.

But a stone was a stone, no matter how unusual or pretty. It was an inanimate object, not a living thing. He'd keep it as a good luck charm—not that he believed in such things—but as for it generating healing energy, well, that was just a lot of hooey.

He set the stone back on the coffee table before heading to the barn to do his evening chores. He'd show it to Cora the next time he saw her.

He awakened the next morning to the sound of a cardinal trilling from the redbud tree growing beside the house and the pungent but not unpleasant scent of cow manure wafting through the open window from the pastures. It was his habit to lie in bed for twenty minutes or so, planning out his day, but this morning needed no planning. He sprang from his bed and quickly slipped into the comfortable old khaki trousers he usually wore when hiking. The blackberry brambles had done a number on his legs, scratching him quite badly in a few places. He didn't intend to let that happen again.

Down in the kitchen, he filled a canteen with water and made a couple of peanut butter and jelly sandwiches. These and a plastic bag of dried cherries and apples he packed in his hip pack before strapping it around his slim waist.

He stopped at the barn to do his morning chores. His horse, Chance, nickered a greeting, and James-Cyrus took the time to scratch the blaze on the old roan's nose as she happily munched on the bucket of oats he gave her. "We'll go out for a ride later, okay girl? Maybe over to Cora's?" The horse, intent on eating her oats, ignored him, and he moved on.

The mice had been in the chicken feed again. Persistent little buggers, he thought, chewing through the heavy plastic bin he'd installed just a few weeks earlier. He didn't wish the mice harm, really—he actually thought they were kind of cute. But he couldn't afford to keep feeding them expensive chicken feed. Maybe he'd have to get a barn cat to chase them away. He refused to think a cat might actually eat the mice. He scooped half a gallon of feed, and exited the back door of the barn to the chicken yard. The birds came running at the sight of him, clucking madly for their breakfast.

Chickens fed, he returned the feed scoop to the barn. He looked guiltily at the soiled hay in Chance's stall, but he was in a hurry. "I'll muck it out for you later, okay, girl? Meanwhile, why don't you spend some time outside today? It's gonna be a beauty." He opened the stall door so she could wander out into the fenced barnyard if the mood struck her.

Before his grandfather died, they had discussed getting a few head of dairy cattle, but now he was glad he didn't have to take the time to milk morning and night. His beef cattle grazed peacefully in the pasture all summer long, and other than occasional veterinary check-ups, required little attention.

Chores complete, he headed for the mountain. This time he did not stop at the cemetery to talk to his grandfather, instead plunging straight into the woods and around the big rock that marked the trail.

Anticipation carried him up the mountain at a much more rapid rate than he had taken a few days earlier, and he had to consciously will himself to slow down so as not to tire out on the steep slope. As on his first forage up the mountain, he stopped to rest at the creek—the little ground squirrel emerged from his den once again, but stopped his scolding as soon as James-Cyrus threw him a handful of dried fruit.

He was sitting with his back to a tree, munching a peanut butter and jelly sandwich and thinking over the events of his last hike up the mountain when, suddenly, every hair on the back of his neck snapped to attention at the sound of branches crackling behind him. The ground squirrel scurried back to his den just as two yearling bear cubs tumbled through the brush. At the sight of James-Cyrus they stopped their playful wrestling and, with sharp cries of alarm, scurried up a witch hazel tree not five feet from where he rested.

Uh, oh, this isn't good. "Where's your mamma, little fellas?" he said softly as he slowly rose and began backing toward the creek.

He was halfway across the water when he heard a loud *huff, huff,* from the brush. He turned and ran just as the enraged mother bear came charging toward the creek.

Reaching the far bank of the creek, James-Cyrus scrambled up the steep bank and leaped on top of an enormous granite boulder jutting out over the water. Grabbing a sturdy branch of driftwood lodged between the boulder and creek bank, he pulled himself up as tall as he could and turned to face the bear.

"Get out of here!" he screamed, jumping up and down and waving the branch high over his head. "You, bear, beat it!"

The bear stopped in her tracks, mid stream. Raising herself up on her hind legs, she huffed again and sniffed at the air. She turned, looking back the way she came, and sniffed again.

Did she lose my scent? he wondered. It didn't seem possible—he was only ten feet from her, and a few feet above her. Bears had bad eyesight, he knew, but their sense of smell was acute.

She turned back toward him, gave one more *huff,* then dropped back on all fours and began overturning stones on the bottom of the creek bed. Every few rocks, the bear would uncover a crawfish or newt and quickly gobble down the treat. Once she uncovered a brook trout's hiding place, but the fish was too quick and managed to elude her razor-sharp claws.

Slowly, James-Cyrus crouched down on the boulder and prepared to slide off the far side, away from the bear. The bear, however, would have none of it, and charged the boulder with a roar. He leaped back to his feet. The bear halted.

"Okay, okay, you're in charge," he said soothingly to the ruffled animal. "I'm not going anywhere."

The bear shook her head, huffed again, and made one last mock charge at the boulder before sauntering back to the tree where her cubs had been watching with what looked to James-Cyrus like rapt fascination. She grunted twice, and the cubs scurried back down the tree. The three disappeared back into the woods.

He waited a couple minutes before scrambling down from his perch. "Well, that was an adventure," he said to the ground squirrel, who had re-emerged from the safety of his hole. "Guess I better remember to wear my bear bells next time."

The squirrel chattered back as if in agreement. James-Cyrus tossed the last dried apple across the river in the squirrel's direction, then slid off the boulder and proceeded up the mountain.

It was an adventure, seeing the bears like that, although he would have preferred if he had stumbled across them accidentally rather than they across him. He'd had at least a dozen encounters with bears while hiking along the Appalachian Trail and on camping trips down in the Smokies. Usually, he could stop and quietly observe them from a safe distance as they browsed for berries or acorns, backing off slowly if his presence appeared to disturb them.

He'd even been charged once before, but he knew that most of the time charges were bluffs, and he'd held his ground, waving his arms and shouting. The bear had backed off. This was the first time he'd ever felt truly threatened, but he knew the sow was just trying to protect her cubs. He didn't take it personally.

The excitement invigorated him, and he whistled an off-key tune as he bounded up the faint trail. He hoped the girl Elizabeth was still at the cabin. He wanted what had happened to be real. "If it wasn't real, you're in serious need of professional help, JC," he said aloud, using the nickname his grandfather bestowed upon him.

Forty minutes later, he reached the clearing. His stomach flip-flopped—whether with excitement or trepidation, James-Cyrus wasn't sure—as he climbed the stone stairs to the cabin and eased open the rusty hinged door.

He stared through a lacy cobweb curtain into an empty, crumbling room.

He dreamed of the cabin that night.

He was sitting on a branch of an enormous chestnut tree at the base of Hoffmann Mountain. It was the night of the new moon, and even the brilliant shards of starlight cast only a weak glow over the mountain and the valley below. Yet he could see as plainly as if the sun were shining directly over his head.

He watched from the safety of the tree as a mother bear ambled through the underbrush, searching for mushrooms, chestnuts, and other delicacies hidden in the leaf litter of the forest floor. Two cubs tumbled along side her, jumping on her and trying to get her to play.

A sudden commotion turned his attention from the bears at the forest's edge to the valley beyond. He could see a man, wild-eyed with panic, running for cover in the woods, two grizzled and dirty men in pursuit; a fugitive about to be snared by bounty hunters. Far behind James-Cyrus could see a man on a horse galloping full speed toward the men.

The smell of fear and tumult of men sent the mother bear chasing her cubs up the tree, where they clung to the branches right next to James-Cyrus, oblivious to his presence. The mother bear grunted, hackles raised, as the pursued man crashed past her through the brush.

"There he is! Up ahead! I've got him!" One of the pursuers, a man in coveralls with a patch over one eye, raised his pistol, took aim, and fired three shots in rapid succession. The pursued man dove into the underbrush.

"You fool! I've knowed women who could shoot better'n you!" the second bounty hunter shouted.

The bear curled her lip back in a silent snarl, waiting.

The second man raised his gun and fired. The bullet found its mark not in the flesh of the pursued man but deep in the shoulder of the mother bear. With the roar of the damned she took off after the shooters.

"Run!" screamed the one-eyed man as he turned and fled, his companion right behind him and the hot breath of the wounded bear closing in with every step.

The men didn't see the horse charging toward them until it was nearly on top of them. The horse reared, hooves thrashing, catching the one-eyed man in the temple and throwing him backwards. His companion dodged to one side, skirting the horse and continuing full speed across the valley. The bear careened around the horse, still in pursuit of the man.

In an instant James-Cyrus found himself in a different tree, in a different place. He was in the large hemlock at the edge of the clearing, the soft yellow glow of a lantern in the window of the cabin beckoning to him like a lighthouse beacon. He started to climb down from the tree, but stopped when he heard the steady clip, clop, clip, clop of a horse as it slowly approached the clearing.

The horse stepped into the clearing, led by a lanky, graying man in worn black trousers and dusty boots. One sleeve of his white shirt was torn away. Slumped across the saddle was a light-skinned black man, the torn-off shirtsleeve wrapped around his head. It was soaked with blood. James-Cyrus knew this was the man on the horse and the fugitive. He also realized he was looking at his great-great-great-grandfather William, returning from riding the circuit.

"Catherine! Elizabeth!" the man shouted as he tied the horse to the railing in front of the house. The door opened, and out rushed two women, one graying like the man, the other young and raven haired. James-Cyrus recognized Elizabeth.

The women helped slide the injured man off the horse, and carried him into the house. Suddenly, James-Cyrus found himself perched on the top rung of the ladder leading to the loft inside the house. He had a clear view of the activity in the room below him: Catherine was gently peeling off the injured man's bandage while Elizabeth retrieved a bowl of water, some rags, and assorted tinctures from a cupboard filled to the brim with mysterious-looking bottles of amber liquids and dried herbs.

"I found him hiding in the bushes, just off the trail at the base of the mountain," the man explained. "I wouldn't have found him at all if the horse hadn't startled when a bear ran across our path. We nearly trampled him."

"And a fortunate thing for him you nearly did; he's been shot, William," Catherine replied, examining the wound on the man's head.

"Looks like it only grazed him, but head wounds bleed so much. Elizabeth, please bring the lantern closer so I can see properly."

Elizabeth picked up the lantern from the table, looking up as she did so. Her eyes widened and she let out a startled gasp. "Cyrus!" Her voice was a coarse whisper, and she slowly reached her hand out toward the ladder.

James-Cyrus stretched to take Elizabeth's hand, but instead awakened to find himself grasping at air in the darkness of his own bedroom.

Chapter 5

Catherine turned and looked at her daughter, "Elizabeth?" she asked, the question in her voice shaking Elizabeth out of her fright.

She looked again at the ladder that led to her loft bedroom, where moments earlier she had been certain Cyrus was sitting, reaching for her hand. But only a shadow danced across the top rungs when she swung the lantern around.

Get a handle on yourself, Elizabeth, she scolded silently. *There's no one there, Cyrus is off fighting...there's...no...one...there!*

Out loud, she said, "Sorry, Mamma. The lantern is hot, I burned myself a bit. I'm fine," she added hastily, seeing her mother's alarmed look.

"Be careful. Here, hold the lantern just there," Catherine said, moving Elizabeth's arm into position so she could see. "William, please get me a fresh bandage and the witch hazel tincture. It's the green one," she said, nodding at one of the bottles Elizabeth had put on the table.

Elizabeth watched as her mother cleaned and rebandaged the wounded man's head. The bleeding had slowed considerably, if not quite stopped.

"We can hide him in the barn," William said. "In the secret room." He turned to his daughter. "Can you go out there and see that the bed is prepared? I'll follow in a few minutes with him, just as soon as your mother is finished."

"Of course, Papa," she said. Lighting another lantern, she slipped out the back door and headed for the barn.

There was nothing remarkable about the structure when viewed from the front. It looked like any normal barn, situated at the edge of the clearing with the thick woods arcing around its back. Only from the inside, and only if one knew where to look, did the barn reveal its secret.

Elizabeth entered and hung her lantern on a peg on the back wall. She counted over five boards to the right of the peg, knelt down and stuck her index finger in a knothole about six inches above the floor. She felt around for only a moment before finding what she searched for. Pushing down the iron pin she felt but could not see, Elizabeth felt the latch release. She stood once again and, pressing hard on the board, shoved the narrow door open into the little room hidden beyond.

She and Mamma had laughed when Papa and Cyrus had built the concealed room, just before Cyrus left to join the Union army. The room was intended to be a place the two women could hide in case trouble came to the clearing while Papa was riding the circuit and Cyrus was off fighting the war, but Elizabeth had thought it quite the folly, for if trouble had arrived in the clearing, she had no qualms at all about shooting a rifle. Besides, the barn was a good fifty feet back from the house. It would have been difficult to slip out the back door and cross the yard to the safety of the barn without being seen. But Papa and Cyrus had been quite insistent there be a hiding place, and the barn was the only logical place to build it. Now, thinking about the injured man inside, Elizabeth was thankful the men had such foresight.

The room was small—only eight feet square—yet comfortably furnished. Elizabeth set down her lantern, then lowered the platform bed that was folded up against the back wall. She pulled a soft feather mattress from a square chest, shaking it hard to fluff it before spreading it over the platform. She added several blankets—nights got cool on the mountain, even in the summer—then grabbed a water pitcher from the small wash stand and ran out to the pump. She neglected to pick up her lantern, but no matter; her eyes adjusted quickly to the dark.

She was halfway back to the barn when the back door of the cabin opened and her father and mother stepped out, half carrying, half dragging the wounded man across the yard. She hurried ahead to put down the water pitcher, then returned to help with the injured man.

"He's starting to come around a bit," Catherine said as they eased him onto the platform bed. It was a tight squeeze, having so many people in the tiny, hidden room. "Elizabeth, please return to the house with your father and fix him something to eat. I'll stay here for a bit just in case he awakens." She covered the man with one of the blankets. "He's going to be weak as a kitten; I don't want to leave him here alone."

William started to protest, but Catherine gently shoved both her husband and her daughter out of the room. "Go on now, get some food and tidy up a bit. Elizabeth, after you've tended to your father, please bring me some broth for our guest. He's going to need nourishment to regain his strength."

William ate two bowls of bean soup and half a pan of cornbread before falling asleep in the rocking chair. Elizabeth covered him with a shawl, then ladled up a mug of bean broth for the injured visitor before once again heading for the barn.

She was surprised to hear her mother's voice as she entered the barn. "Our guest has awakened," Catherine announced cheerfully, taking the broth from Elizabeth. "Malachi, this is my daughter, Elizabeth. Elizabeth, Malachi."

The man tipped his head toward Elizabeth. "How do you do, miss." His attempt at a smile turned to a grimace, and he reached for his head. "Ouch. It hurts to move much."

"Then hold still," Catherine said briskly, fussing with the pillow supporting Malachi's bandaged head. "You drink this broth down, then get some sleep. It's very late. You're safe here—no one can find you."

"I owe you—" Malachi began, but Catherine cut him off.

"You owe us nothing, for now. There's plenty of time to talk when you are feeling restored." She smiled, and slipped from the room. "Come, Elizabeth."

They closed the door to the secret room and returned to the cabin.

Catherine had been right about there being plenty of time to talk. Malachi was weak from blood loss from the bullet wound. His ankle, too, was injured, although Catherine was satisfied it was only a sprain and nothing more serious. "You'll be back to normal in no time," she assured him.

Elizabeth found herself making up excuses to visit Malachi in the barn. She changed the bandage on his head wound, brought him food and tea, and sat with him for hours, talking. She couldn't take her eyes off him when they were together. His skin was the color of tea with plenty of milk in it—a colored man, without a doubt, yet fairer of complexion than many white men she knew. His eyes were the color of roasted chestnuts and shone as though flecked with mica. She judged him to be a few years older than herself, twenty-three or twenty-four, perhaps, and by far the most beautiful man she had ever laid eyes on.

She was dying with curiosity about him—who he was, how he had gotten injured, what he was doing, hiding in the brush on Hoffmann Mountain. She wondered if he was a runaway slave. That would explain why he had been hiding, but if he was a runaway, wouldn't bounty hunters be after him?

"There are far more runaway slaves than there are bounty hunters chasing them," her father had said when she asked him about the stranger recuperating in their barn. "If that wasn't the case, no slave would dare make a run for freedom because he'd be caught for sure." He gave her a feeble smile.

"But Papa, if he's run away he's not safe—"

He put his finger gently to her mouth, shushing her. "Don't worry about Malachi, and please, sweetheart, don't ask him too many questions. Let him recover his strength in peace. He's safe here, at least for now."

So Elizabeth tried not to worry about the handsome stranger, and obeyed her father by not asking Malachi too many questions about his past. Instead, she talked to him about her life in the cabin on Hoffmann Mountain. She told him about Cyrus, off fighting for the Yankees despite being a Virginian. She talked about the books her father brought her whenever he came home from riding the circuit. "He has a cousin who is a merchant in Richmond," she said. "He used to be able to get all the latest books, from England, even, but Papa says it is getting harder and harder because of the war." She showed Malachi the thick volume her father had given her a few days earlier, *Silas Marner* by George Eliot.

Malachi reached for the book and fanned through the pages. "I read Eliot's *The Mill on the Floss*," he said. "She's a gifted writer."

"She?"

"Didn't you know George Eliot is a woman?" Malachi sounded surprised. "Her real name is Mary Anne Evans. She took the name George Eliot because women have trouble getting published under their own names. Seems writing is supposed to be a man's profession."

"Women aren't supposed to be able to do a lot of things, but we do them anyway," Elizabeth said, resigned. "My mother is a gifted healer, but no one would ever dare suggest she could be a doctor."

He reached up and touched his bandaged head. "I'd be the first to say she'd make a fine doctor. I'd probably be dead from blood loss or an infection if your father hadn't found me and your mother hadn't known how to treat my wound." He returned to the book, skimming through the pages.

"Malachi, how did you learn how to read?" Elizabeth could contain her curiosity no longer. "I thought it was against the law for a...well, you know, for—"

"For a colored man to learn how to read?" Malachi finished her sentence. "It is." He shut the book with a heavy sigh. "The mistress of the plantation I used to, um, live on taught me to read. There was a wonderful library in the big house, with more books than you could possibly imagine. When I was a boy I thought she had every book ever written."

He reached for the glass of water sitting on the chest next to the platform bed and took a long drink. Elizabeth waited, silent, hoping he would continue.

"Anyway, she caught me looking at one of the books when I was about nine or so. I was supposed to be dusting them, but I just couldn't resist taking a peek. I thought she'd tar and feather me when she caught me, but instead she locked the door to the library and asked me if I'd like to learn what was in those books.

"Over the course of the next year, we'd sneak in reading lessons as often as we could. We didn't dare when her husband was home, but he was away frequently, and she would give me lessons then. She said I was a quick study."

He fell silent for a moment, stroking the fine leather cover of the George Eliot book. "She died in childbirth a year or so later. I was older by then, big enough to work the fields, so that was the end of my education. Her husband never did find out she'd taught me to read, although I think he suspected."

"So you weren't able to read anymore books?" Elizabeth tried to imagine what it would be like, not being able to read her books. The idea horrified her.

"Not exactly." Malachi grinned. "He kept up the library for show, buying new books when they were printed. He liked to entertain in there, bragging to all his gentlemen friends about his fine library. But he never read himself. The missus told me once he couldn't read very well, that the letters seemed to get all scrambled up on him. One of the house workers used to leave the library window open a crack for me at night, so I could sneak in and borrow books. He never noticed."

He set the copy of *Silas Marner* on the chest. "That's how I got to read *The Mill on the Floss*. It was the last book I read before I left."

"I'm glad you told me, Malachi," Elizabeth said, suddenly feeling both shy and a bit flustered. "I've wanted to ask what your story was, but Papa told me not to ask too many questions."

He smiled. "I'll tell you the rest, but right now I'm feeling pretty tuckered out. How about you telling me something about you, so we're even?" He leaned back against the wall and closed his eyes.

"A story about me? I'm not very interesting," she said.

"Everyone has a story, Elizabeth. What's life, after all, if it isn't a series of stories? Just pick something."

There was one story, but she'd never spoken to anyone outside the family about it. It was a story her father and mother had told her when she was fifteen, and she had been discouraged from talking about it after that time despite the thousand questions the story raised. She looked at Malachi, so beautiful, so trusting, sharing his story with her. I can tell this man, she realized. He will understand.

"Catherine isn't really my mother," she began, hesitating only a moment. Malachi opened his eyes again, his look urging her to continue. "She really is my aunt.

Corrine, my birth mother, disappeared when I was only a few weeks old."

She told him what she knew, a sketchy account of what happened, at best. "Papa and Catherine were outside. Cyrus was just a toddler, and he said she just stepped out the front door and vanished into thin air. They searched the mountain, but never found a trace of her. Catherine stayed on to help care for us—that was why she was here to begin with; she helped my mother with birthing me—and Papa married her about a year later."

"Did they ever figure out what happened to her?"

Elizabeth shook her head. "Papa thought perhaps she was kidnapped by Indians, but that sort of thing hadn't happened in these parts in decades. And Cyrus insisted she just disappeared. There one moment, gone the next. He didn't say anything about her being kidnapped. And Papa and Mamma—Catherine—would have heard the commotion if she had screamed. It's all just one big mystery."

"Strange things happen in this world that are beyond our ability to explain," Malachi said, trying unsuccessfully to stifle a yawn.

"I've kept you from resting too long." Elizabeth rose from the stool she'd been perched on, stretching as she did so. The little room was warm and cramped. She needed to get out in the fresh air. "Oh, I almost forgot! Mamma said if you feel up to it, later you can get some air outside. She just wants to wait until Papa gets home so he can help you walk on that bad ankle."

"I'm about to go stark raving mad cooped up inside like this," Malachi admitted. He picked up her book. "Here, don't forget this."

"Why don't you keep it for now to read? I've got a Wilkie Collins book I can read, *The Woman in White.* I'm a bit surprised Papa brought it to me. He said it created quite the scandal in England." She grinned.

Malachi returned the grin. "Well, George Eliot created quite the scandal herself, living with a man she wasn't married to." He took the proffered book. "Thank you, Elizabeth. You're very kind."

Elizabeth slipped out of the room, then ran across the barn floor and out into the sunshine. She didn't know when she last felt this happy. She knew only that spending time with Malachi made her feel things, think things, she'd never felt or thought before. And while she had very little experience with men—none, really, unless you counted the time the blacksmith's son kissed her behind the boxwood hedge next to his father's shop—she knew what those feelings and thoughts meant.

The thought made her shiver, both with delight and with fear.

Chapter 6

Malachi's wounds healed rapidly, and by the end of the week he was joining the family in the cabin for meals, and helping out with simple chores. He groomed the horse, and cleaned and oiled all the garden tools. He swept the barn with such vigor and enthusiasm the broomstick snapped in two, and he spent an entire afternoon and evening whittling a new one, carving an elaborate vine design up its length and topping it with a delicate morel mushroom tip, to Elizabeth's great delight. She sat with him while he carved, and read aloud from *Silas Marner*.

She was especially grateful when he shooed her from the garden when she was performing the unsavory chore of picking tomato worms off plants. She wasn't one of those squeamish girls who shrieked at the sight of a bug or a mouse, but tomato worms were just plain disgusting, she thought.

She watched, puzzled, as he began to dig a series of holes around the perimeter of the garden, and bury old, chipped and cracked medicine bottles he found in a corner of the barn so only their narrow rims stuck above the ground. He sang as he worked:

> *When the sun comes up and the first quail calls,*
> *Follow the drinking gourd.*
> *For the old man is a-waiting to carry you to freedom,*
> *If you follow the drinking gourd.*
>
> *The mountains make a very good road,*
> *The dead trees show you the way,*
> *Left foot, peg foot, traveling on,*
> *Follow the drinking gourd…*

"It's a beautiful song, Malachi, but what does it mean?"

Malachi placed a bottle in the hole he'd dug while singing and patted the dirt firmly around it. "It's a song taught to those who are still captive but who are planning to escape," he said. "It tells them how to reach the safety of the north."

"I don't understand. What does a drinking gourd have to do with escaping to freedom?"

"It's symbolic, it isn't a real gourd." Malachi took the spade and began digging another hole. "The drinking gourd refers to the big dipper. It tells runners to follow the big dipper, and it'll lead them north to freedom."

He put down the spade and motioned to Elizabeth to hand him another bottle. "The second verse advises them to stick to the mountains, where they can hide easily. Plus, there are so many streams running through the mountains its easy to walk in the water. Bloodhounds can't follow someone through water."

Bottle planted in the dirt, Malachi began digging another hole. "Of course, this isn't how the song was first written. I learned the original words from a man I met up with a while back, a man from Alabama. That one was for slaves escaping from Alabama up to Ohio. It tells them to follow the rivers to freedom. We just changed a few words so it'd work for this neck of the woods."

Bottles planted, he stepped back and cocked his head to the side. "Be still now, and listen."

A soft breeze wafted across the clearing, and as it blew across the bottles, they sang a cacophonic symphony of whistles and sighs.

"The noise will keep the rabbits and raccoons out," he explained. "Of course, it only helps when there's a breeze blowing."

Elizabeth clapped her hands with delight. "How wonderful! Really, quite ingenious."

"Delightful now," he grinned. "There's not much of a breeze. Wait until you have a good gust blowing through here and you may find yourself digging them up just to save your ears."

A catbird called from the hemlock tree at the edge of the forest. Malachi jumped, his eyes scanning the perimeter of the clearing. Elizabeth followed his eyes, sensing his alarm.

"What's the matter? What are you looking for?"

Apparently satisfied nothing was lurking at the forest edge, Malachi relaxed. "Catbird. They make me jumpy when they get too close."

"Whatever for?" Elizabeth asked. "I think they're charming. They always keep me company when I'm walking through the forest."

"That's exactly why I pay close attention to them. They can give warning that someone is coming. The only problem with them is, they can't tell us if it's a friend or enemy." He picked up the spade he had been using to bury the bottles in the garden. "Let me put this away. Then, if you have a few minutes to listen, I need to talk to you and your folks about a few things."

"What is it, Malachi? Something's wrong. I can sense it."

Malachi began picking off clumps of soil that stubbornly clung to the spade. He didn't look at her, and Elizabeth was about to give up waiting for his reply when he spoke.

"I'm leaving tonight, Elizabeth. Soon as it gets good and dark, I have to be on my way."

"But why?" she burst out, a little louder, a little angrier than she'd intended. She softened her tone and repeated her question. "Why?"

"It's not safe for me to stay here any longer. Not safe for me, and not safe for you or your folks for me to be here.

Besides, I have work to do. People depend on me." He started walking toward the barn. Elizabeth followed.

"But why isn't it safe? What aren't you telling me? Why do you want to leave?"

He didn't answer her until they'd reach the dark coolness of the barn. He carefully placed the spade in its place among the other tools. Only then did he face her.

"Elizabeth, there are things you don't know about me. Things I've not shared with you because we were strangers. It's not easy for me to trust strangers, especially…"

Her face grow hot. "Especially what? Especially white strangers? Or is it because I'm a woman?"

He sighed. "Of course it's hard for me to trust white folks. Look at me, Elizabeth!" he grabbed her by the arm, lifting her chin with his other hand so she was forced to look him in the eye. "But that isn't the issue here. Of course I trust you. I trust you all."

She felt tears building, and vainly tried to keep them from spilling down her face. "Then why are you leaving?" she asked softly.

His look was filled with such tenderness Elizabeth thought, for a fleeting moment, that he was going to kiss her. She wanted him to kiss her, she realized.

Instead, he released his grasp. "Let's go into the house," he suggested. "I'm going to tell you, but it isn't just my story to tell. You may as well hear it all at once, and he was going to tell you and Catherine tonight anyway."

"Who?" Elizabeth asked, confused.

"Your father. We didn't just meet when he found me wounded, Elizabeth. We've known each other ever since he helped me escape from...escape to freedom."

"I was just fixing us a pot of tea," Catherine said when Elizabeth and Malachi entered the cabin. "Your father has some big secret he wants to share with us." She winked at her daughter. "Secrets in the house, and here it isn't even Christmas."

"It's not that sort of secret, Catherine," William said. "This is a serious matter that no longer affects only me."

"Who wants pound cake with their tea?" Not bothering to wait for an answer, Elizabeth took some plates from the cupboard and cut generous slices of cake for the two men, and thin slices for herself and her mother.

"Well, get on with it then, William." Catherine poured the tea as Elizabeth placed the cake on the table. "What's all the mystery?"

"Malachi said you knew him, Papa," Elizabeth said. "Why didn't you tell us when you brought him here you were already friends?"

"I was protecting you," William answered. "But I think it would be easier if Malachi told the story. I might leave something out. Besides," he redirected his gaze from Elizabeth toward Malachi, "I don't want to say anything you don't want shared."

Malachi took a bite of cake. "Umm, This is really good. I think at this point, if you're sure about what we discussed last evening, William, that they should know the whole story."

"What whole story?" Elizabeth was beginning to feel quite exasperated by the men's cryptic speech. "Just tell us!"

"I think to understand why I'm here, and what William and I have been so secretive about, you need to know my story, from the very beginning," Malachi said. "I told you already, Elizabeth, how I learned to read."

She nodded. "Yes, and I told Mamma and Papa. I thought it was so…courageous of you to learn, considering the circumstances."

"There's nothing courageous about wanting to learn. It's a basic human right. But I know you mean that as a compliment, so I thank you.

"A few years back, I decided to try to pass on what she had taught me to the other slaves. I'd hold a kind of school during the night, after all the lights were out in the big house. I had about a dozen students, ranging from an eight-year-old girl to a man of fifty, all giving up an hour or two of badly needed rest in order to learn to read.

"All went well with the school until a little over a year ago, when one of the house workers got caught browsing through a book in the library, whispering the words aloud as she struggled to read them. The plantation owner, a man by the name of John Bryan, couldn't read very well himself—I told you how words would get jumbled up when he read— but he could make enough out to realize she was, indeed, reading the text. He threatened to flay her inch by inch if she didn't tell him who taught her to read."

Catherine shuddered. "Malachi, how awful. What did you do?" She reached over and refilled his tea cup, then William's. Elizabeth's tea sat untouched and cold.

"Another house worker, Aaron was his name, overheard her tell Bryan it was me. Aaron sneaked out of the house and came to find me in the orchard, where I was working, and warn me trouble was brewing."

He fell silent for a moment, taking the last bite of his pound cake and finishing off his tea before continuing.

"I ran like a rabbit being chased by a fox. Didn't get to go back for my few possessions, or to say good-bye to anyone. I just took off. I knew if I didn't I'd be a dead man or worse."

"Worse?" Elizabeth gasped. "What could be worse?"

"Sometimes torture is worse than death," William said quietly.

Malachi nodded in agreement. "I'll not brighten your day with tales the atrocities one human being is capable of inflicting on another. But your father is right. Death is infinitely preferable to torture.

"I was lucky, the day I ran. It was late in the day, and by the time Bryan realized I was gone, it was dark. Easier to hide at night, and safer to travel."

"But where does William fit into this story, Malachi?" Catherine asked. "He told me, just before you two came in from the barn, that he helped you escape."

"That's right," Malachi continued. "That first night, I ran until I was about to drop from exhaustion. I ran so long I lost track of my senses, and stumbled into his camp site."

"Lucky for Malachi, it was one of those evenings when I wasn't offered a bed along my circuit," said William, picking up the tale. "It was a beautiful, clear night, so I decided not to waste money on an inn. I was plumb near asleep when suddenly he came stumbling into my camp. He quite literally tripped right over me and fell."

Catherine smiled. "I can't imagine who was the more startled: you at being tripped over, William; or you, Malachi, at suddenly stumbling over him."

"Malachi, by far," William said. "He was so exhausted, he just looked at me and said something like, 'Please. Have mercy.' I assured him he was safe with me, that I meant him no harm."

"William helped me get to West Virginia," Malachi said. "He borrowed a wagon to hide me, hitched up that old nag of his, and drove me right over the border. He saved my life."

"Where I thought you'd stay, safe and sound," William grumbled.

"Why did you come back, Malachi?" Elizabeth asked, puzzled. "If you made it to freedom, why did you risk your life coming back?"

"He's been helping others reach freedom, that's why," William said. "He's risked his own freedom to help people who want the same liberties the three of us have always enjoyed." He reached out and took his wife's hand in one hand, his daughter's in the other. "And so have I."

The magnitude of what her father was saying suddenly dawned on Elizabeth. "The underground railroad," she whispered.

"Yes."

Elizabeth looked at her mother. Catherine looked as dumbfounded as she herself felt. Her father, working as a...what did they call themselves?...she'd read about it in one of the copies of *The Liberator* her father had brought home a few months back...conductors, that was it. Her father, a conductor on the underground railroad, helping Malachi and others like him cross the border into a free state, risking his life, risking being caught up in the skirmishes of war that were ravaging Virginia.

She jumped up from the table and threw her arms around her father. "I'm so proud of you, Papa!" she said. "Really, really proud of you."

She let go of her father and turned to Malachi. "You too, Malachi," she said shyly. You've got ever so much to lose if you get caught."

"Your father has a lot to lose, too," he answered. "The Fugitive Slave Act prohibits aiding slaves who are running. Your father could go to jail."

"Well, he'd only go to jail if he got caught, and my husband is much too smart to get caught," Catherine said.

"We nearly did get caught," William said, grimly. He quickly filled the women in on what had happened the night Malachi arrived at the cabin. "If the horse hadn't kicked and killed the one man chasing Malachi, and if the bear hadn't sent the other one screaming off down the valley, we could have been in serious trouble," he said.

"But Papa, you said there weren't any bounty hunters after him," Elizabeth protested. "You said he was safe here!"

William smiled tenderly at his daughter. "I didn't want you worrying needlessly when there was nothing we could do about the situation. Malachi was too injured to move safely."

He pushed his chair back from the table and stretched his long legs out to the side. "I knew those bounty hunters. Ephram and Bertram Hammer, their names are. They've been after Malachi for months now. I've managed to steer them off on a couple wild goose chases when they came sniffing too close, but this time they somehow got wind of where Malachi was before I could do anything about it. By the time I learned what they were up to, it was almost too late."

"But dear, won't they be back?" Catherine's usually composed face looked ashen with fear.

"Well, not Bertram," William replied. "I dragged him into the woods and left him for the scavengers. Ephram, though, will probably be back as soon as he can round up someone else to help him. With all the skirmishing going on down in the valley, I reckon it'll be a while before he gets back home, let alone makes his way back to where he lost track of Malachi."

"What ever happened to Aaron and the woman Mister Bryan found reading that day you ran, Malachi? Do you know?" Malachi's grimace confirmed Elizabeth's feeling this was a question best left unasked, and she immediately regretting letting her curiosity get the better of her common sense.

"I heard Bryan sold her to a land owner in Mississippi. He sold her, but not her three children or her husband."

"How awful."

"She's still alive, as far as I know. Aaron, though, was tied to a post out in a field and flayed, an inch at a time. I heard it took him nearly a week to die."

They sat in silence, Elizabeth staring into her cup of now cold tea, struggling with the anger she felt welling up inside her. *Why can't people treat one another civilly?* she wondered. *Why do some people think they're better than other simply because of the color of their skin?*

By the time the moon rose over the clearing on the mountain, Malachi was ready to go. "Walk to the edge of the clearing with me," he asked Elizabeth.

They walked without speaking, yet the clearing was far from silent. Cicadas and katydids sang from every tree, drowning out even the music of water dancing among the rocks of the creek. Her sadness over his departure was tempered with the joy of knowing he would now be a regular visitor to the cabin, as well as a healthy dose of fear for his safety.

"Be careful," she whispered as he gathered her into his arms. "If anything happened to you…"

"Nothing is going to happen to me," he said, hugging her with such ferocity she could barely breathe. "Remember, a lantern in the front window on the night of the moon's first quarter means it's safe for me to come."

She could not respond; her words were smothered by his kiss.

Then he was gone.

Chapter 7

Night fell over Hoffman Mountain like a comfortable shawl, draping the cabin in darkness.   Elizabeth loved the night. She loved the way the stars lit up the clearing like so many far-away fireflies, how the moon beamed down at her like a benevolent protectress smiling at a beloved child. Despite childhood stories of the man in the moon, she always thought of the moon as a feminine spirit, closely attuned to her own emotions. When the moon was full she was full of energy, passion, and emotion; when the moon was new she was more introspective, quiet and reserved.

Tonight was the night of the first quarter, a night that always filled Elizabeth with a mixture of excited expectation and gnawing fear.   If a package was going to arrive, it would be tonight.   She lit a kerosene lantern and placed it in the front window, the sign that all was safe and it was okay for the fugitives to approach the cabin.

She wished her mother was home.   It was unusual for her to be gone so many days attending a birth, but sometimes, if more than one woman was due to deliver within the course of a few days, Catherine stayed in the valley for a week or longer. They never knew how long she would be gone when she packed her midwifing bag and headed down the narrow dirt trail that led to the valley.

Of course, if a package came tonight, she wouldn't be alone. And if that happened, if a frightened but determined fugitive slave made his or her way through the darkness to the cabin in a desperate bid for freedom, Malachi would come, too.

The past months had been the most frightening and the most glorious of her life. Frightening, for now she worried not only about her brother off fighting the war and her father out ministering to soldiers on the battlefield, but also about Malachi, risking his life as he accompanied frightened runaways to the safety of the cabin, then on across the mountains to freedom in the north. Glorious, because she had fallen deeply in love with the soft-spoken, intelligent freedom fighter with skin the color of milky tea and eyes the color of roasted chestnuts.

And Malachi loved her, too. He had told her as much the last time he was at the cabin.

Shielding her eyes from the lantern's light, she pressed her face to the pane and peered out the window. The bear and cubs that had raided their blackberry bushes a few days earlier had returned. Enchanted, Elizabeth watched them a few minutes while they searched for more berries. Finding none, they soon melted back into the forest.

"Best get moving here, Elizabeth," she chided herself. It was the first time she'd spoken aloud all day, and the sound of her voice comforted her. There was work to be done to prepare for the weary travelers who would rest here for a night or two before moving on to the next station on the underground railroad.

After stirring the kettle of bean soup she had set to simmer on the hearth, Elizabeth busied herself filling a basket with candles, a jar of water, bread, dried strips of beef, and, after only a moment's hesitation, a small jar of blackberry preserves. Lighting another lantern, she then headed across the clearing toward the barn.

Elizabeth set the basket of food on the wash stand. Taking a broom from the barn, she swept the cobwebs from the corners of the hidden room, and brushed the dust from the rustic plank floor. She folded down the platform bed, then pulled the feather mattress from the storage chest. Fluffing it as best she could, she placed it on the platform. It was a warm evening; one blanket would probably suffice. She pulled out the nicest one and spread it across the mattress. After placing the candles in the two wall sconces, she gave the room a satisfied look and slipped back into the barn.

Remembering the bear and her cubs lurking in the woods nearby, Elizabeth ran across the clearing to the cabin. She wasn't ordinarily afraid of a bear, but she was acutely aware a mother bear who feared for her cubs' safety would not hesitate to kill.

The door swung slowly open as she neared the cabin, stopping Elizabeth dead in her tracks. She hesitated only long enough to set down her lantern and basket.

"Mamma, you're home!" she cried, and ran into her mother's open arms.

Catherine folded her arms around her daughter and gave her a quick squeeze. "Yes, I'm home, and look who has brought me safely back!"

Elizabeth let go of her mother and peered into the dim cabin.

"Malachi!" It was all she could do to keep herself from throwing herself into his arms.

"Elizabeth. We were just coming out to look for you." Malachi smiled warmly. "We were a little worried when you weren't here."

"I was in the barn, getting things ready," she explained. "Are you hungry? I've made bean soup."

"Thank you, dear." Catherine stepped outside the door and retrieved Elizabeth's basket and lantern. "I am hungry, and tired as well." She set the lantern on the table and placed the basket on the shelf. "I was most fortunate Malachi somehow learned of my whereabouts and was there to escort me home this evening. Otherwise I would have had to remain in the valley for yet another night." She frowned, knitting her brows together so tightly they became as one. "I don't like leaving you up here alone for so long, Elizabeth."

Elizabeth took three bowls from the cupboard. "I'm not afraid to be alone. Besides, I know how to use that." She nodded in the direction of the rifle that leaned against the wall near the front door. "But I am glad to have you home, Mamma. You too, Malachi."

She busied herself with brewing sassafras tea while Catherine and Malachi washed up. What she told them was true: she wasn't afraid of being alone on the mountain. Still, it did get lonely sometimes when her mother was away. Papa hadn't been home in weeks, and Cyrus had been gone more than year. And it *had* been more than a year—she had, by this time, convinced herself his strange appearance at the cabin was nothing more than a dream. How else could she explain his disappearing as quickly as he appeared? She knew she wouldn't tell her mother, but wondered if she should tell Malachi about it. Would he take her seriously, or think she was going mad?

A soft rap on the front door jarred her out of her musings. *Tap, tap... taptaptap... tap.* She froze, holding her breath as she waited for the signal to repeat. *Tap, tap... taptaptap... tap.*

Malachi signaled her to pick up the rifle as he quietly approached the door. Elizabeth raised the gun to her shoulder and took aim as Malachi cautiously swung the door open.

"It's all right, Elizabeth, put the gun down." Malachi reached out into the darkness and shepherded in a frightened-looking woman.

The woman looked to be about seventeen—not much more than a girl, really, Elizabeth thought. She was wearing baggy trousers and a ragged overblouse. She was barefooted, and her feet looked bloody and raw. Elizabeth recognized the shadow of a man escorting her. It was Jeremiah, Malachi's cousin.

"Please, won't you come in and rest for a while?" Catherine asked him. "Have a bowl of soup with us."

The shadow took the hat from his head and clutched it tightly. "Thank you kindly, ma'am, but I must be on my way." He turned to the girl. "Flora, this here is Malachi, and this is Miz Catherine and her daughter Miz Elizabeth. They'll help you now. You listen to Malachi, do what he says, and you'll be just fine."

Flora nodded mutely. After murmuring a few words to Malachi, Jeremiah turned and dissolved into the blackness.

Catherine turned to Flora. "Please, sit down here," she urged, leading Flora to a chair. "Let me have a look at your feet. Elizabeth, get me some clean rags from the cupboard. Malachi, would you please pour me some hot water from the tea kettle."

Gently, Catherine washed Flora's tattered, blistered feet. "We must try to find a pair a shoes that fit you before you go on," she said, patting one foot dry before turning her attention to the other. "Your feet are small, like Elizabeth's. I think she may have an old pair of boots that will work for you."

While Catherine washed Flora's feet clean, Elizabeth went to a cabinet and rummaged around through the bottles and jars contained within. Finding the one she wanted, she took another clean rag and soaked it with the clear, fragrant liquid from the bottle.

"Tincture of witch hazel," she explained, daubing the medicine on Flora's feet. Flora gritted her teeth and let out a sharp gasp.

"I'm sorry," Elizabeth apologized. "I know it stings, but it will help prevent infection. Your feet will heal better."

"It's okay, miss," Flora whispered. "Thanks for yer kindness." She smiled shyly. "I never had no white folk treat me so nice before."

"I'm so sorry," Elizabeth apologized again, although this time she wasn't sure what she was apologizing for. For the bad behavior of the white race, she supposed.

After they had all eaten their fill of the bean soup Elizabeth had prepared, they sat at the table and listened to Flora's story.

"I was born down in Georgia, but my master gived me to his brother as a Christmas present when I was 'bout eight years old." Flora spoke softly, but in so melodious a voice Elizabeth fancied the girl singing her story. "I didn't know what was happenin' to me 'til I got ripped from my mamma's arms and dragged kickin' and screamin' into the wagon that brought me north to Virginia. I never seen my mamma again. Don't know 'xactly what happened to her, but I heared she died not long after."

Flora stopped to take a sip of her sassafras tea. "This here's good tea, miss. Good soup, too. Anyways, things wasn't too bad for me at first at White Haven—that was the name of the place I was took. I helped Cook in the kitchen, and emptied the chamber pots and kept the wash pitchers filled with clean water. Nuthin' too hard. Got enough to eat and a warm enough bed to sleep in. Better'n some folks get treated, I know.

"Master's wife died 'bout two years ago. Got the consumption, and coughed herself right into the grave.

Master just 'bout went crazy with grief. I felt real sorry for him, at first, 'cause he and the missus was real close.

"Two weeks after she died, I went in his room to get the chamber pot. I didn't think he was in there—I didn't see him, or I wouldn't have gone in."

She paused for a long moment, eyes closed.

"Flora, if it's too painful, you needn't tell us more." Catherine lay a gentle hand on the girl's arm.

"No ma'am, I's fine." She took another sip of her tea.

"He shut the door behinds me and grabbed me, puttin' his hand over my mouth so's I couldn't scream. Then he threw me down on the floor and..." She gulped, tears welling in her eyes. "My master threw me on the floor and forced hisself on me." The wells overflowed, and Elizabeth felt her own tears trickle down her cheek.

Flora wiped the tears away with an angry swipe of the hand. "After that, he used to call me to his room whenever he wanted to have his way with me. It hurt somethin' awful, and I was so ashamed. I was glad my mamma wasn't there. I was glad she was dead.

"Afore I knowed it, I was carryin' a child. That made him angry. 'I'm gonna beat that baby right out of you,' he said, and lawdy, he done did it, too. She was born alive, but she died the next day. She was jes' too small."

Flora pulled herself tall, and her voice took on a defiant tone. "I made up my mind the day my baby died I was gonna run away. And now here I is. I'm gonna go to Cincinnati, Ohio, and get me a real job. I'm goin' to be a free woman."

When Flora finished her story, she and Malachi bid Catherine and Elizabeth good night and headed for the barn. Flora would sleep in the hidden room; Malachi always slept in the hayloft, so he could keep an eye out and his ears open for the sound of trouble. There was little to worry about, Elizabeth knew. The cabin was in so remote a location it was considered one of the safest havens on the underground railroad.

She bid her mother good night and climbed the ladder to her sleeping loft. She hoped Malachi would stay an extra day. With Flora's feet so terribly injured, perhaps he would deem it safer to stay and let them heal rather than try to run with her barely able to walk.

She fell asleep, hoping.

The sun was no more than a dim, glowing promise in the eastern sky when she awakened the next morning. Elizabeth peeked out the tiny window above her writing desk in the loft, straining to see through the dim morning light. Her eyes searched the clearing, pausing at the faint shadow beneath the hemlock tree. A smile danced across her face.

She slipped out of her nightgown and into her blue calico dress. She didn't bother with her boots—it was summertime, and her feet much preferred the feeling of cool damp earth tickling her toes than hard shoe leather.

She climbed down the ladder, stretching carefully past the third rung to the second. The third rung squeaked loudly, and she didn't wish to awaken her mother. Tiptoeing to the back door, she eased it open just enough to slip through and into the chill morning air.

She flew across the yard toward the hemlock tree, and into Malachi's waiting arms. He held her tightly for a moment, then taking her face in his hands, kissed her gently.

"I was afraid you wouldn't wake up early enough to meet me," he murmured. "Don't know what I would've done if you hadn't come soon."

"I hardly slept last night, I was so happy to see you," she replied, turning her lips to his for another kiss. "I've missed you so much."

"I missed you, too." Malachi took Elizabeth by the hand and led her past the hemlock to the bank of the creek beyond. "Let's sit by the creek and talk."

"Did Flora sleep last night?" Elizabeth gathered her skirt around her as they sank down on a patch of soft moss.

"I reckon she did. I didn't hear a peep out of her once I got her settled in the room."

"I'm glad." Elizabeth's stomach growled, and she wished she'd thought to bring some bread and jam with her for them to share. She didn't dare go back for it now, for fear of awakening her mother. Besides, Malachi would probably be leaving in a few hours. Every moment spent with him was valuable.

As if reading her mind, Malachi said, "Flora's feet are pretty torn up. I think it best we stay until tomorrow, if it's all right with you and Catherine."

Her heart leapt with joy. "You know it's all right, but Malachi, is it safe?"

He frowned. "It's never safe. But it's safer for her here than to get caught out in the woods somewhere because she can't make it to the next safe house. I got ahold of a paper yesterday, and I didn't see anything in the paper about Flora, so either that scum hasn't bothered posting a reward for her or he's not smart enough to realize she's gone."

"Do you really think her owner wouldn't notice her missing, after he…after what he did to her?"

Malachi took Elizabeth's hand in his own. "She's a human being, Elizabeth. He didn't own her—no man can ever really own another, no matter what the law says."

Elizabeth blushed at his gentle rebuke. "You're right. I didn't mean—"

"I know. You're forgiven."

He kissed her again, more passionately than before, and a delicious ache arose deep within her She longed for him to place his hands on her breast, to relieve the ache his kisses inspired.

Reluctantly, she pulled away. They sat in silence, listening to the waltz of water tumbling over the rocks in the creek bed and a chickadee scolding overhead. It was rapidly getting light, and soon Elizabeth would have to return to the cabin lest her mother awaken and worry about her.

She broke the silence, intending to say her good-byes. She posed him a question instead. "Malachi, was a reward ever offered for your capture?"

He grimaced. "Money's a funny thing. Seems those who have little of it freely give it away, and those with a whole lot of it hold onto it like it was a ticket to heaven. I was the best worker my so-called master had. I could push a plow, pick peaches or cotton, or work in the big house with equal skill, and get my work done twice as quickly as any other slave. But in the end, when I up and left, he offered only a fifty dollar reward for my return." Bitter laughter spilled from his throat. "I don't know why I let that bother me. But it seems I'd have been worth at least a couple of hundred."

"You shouldn't joke so."

Malachi quit laughing and looked at Elizabeth soberly. "To tell you the truth, I'm not sure but what he wasn't glad I ran off. With me gone, there was no one to teach the rest of the workers to read."

He stood up, and reached down to help her to her feet. "Education is the key to freedom, Elizabeth. The white man knows that, and keeps the colored man ignorant in order to control him." He pulled her into his arms and held her close.

"The day's coming, though, when the colored man will be free. Free to get an education, free to live where and as he pleases. I want to be there when that day comes. I want to be free to live out in the open, not sneaking through the woods, hiding all the time."

"That's what Cyrus is fighting for, Malachi. It's what we're all fighting for, in whatever way we can."

"Trouble is, even once we've won our freedom, I still won't be free, and neither will you."

She pulled away so she could look him in the eye. "I don't understand what you mean."

His face hardened, and a bitter glint shrouded the desire that only moments before had made his eyes light up when he looked at her.

"Tell me, Elizabeth. Do you believe that once this war is over, you and I will be free to be together?"

Elizabeth paused. His question was one she had often asked herself. In her dreams, she and Malachi were together, married and raising a family right in the cabin on Hoffmann Mountain. She couldn't imagine any other life. But dreams were just that. They weren't real, and as much as she wanted the war to end, as much as she wanted Malachi to be free and safe and her brother home, in her heart she feared when the war ended, no matter which side won, her dream would shatter and she'd lose Malachi forever.

"Mamma and Papa would understand. They'd have to," she said fiercely. "We love each other. They'll see that. They probably already see that."

"But if the laws don't change, we still won't be allowed to marry. Freedom comes in varying degrees, and freedom from slavery doesn't mean freedom to marry outside one's race. And even if the law did change, peoples' attitudes...what are you grinning at?"

"You. What you just said. Is that what you want, Malachi? Do you want to marry me?"

He raised her hand to his lips and kissed it tenderly. "I want to marry you as much as I want the sun to rise tomorrow morning."

"Maybe there's a way. Maybe Papa would marry us."

"Maybe he would and maybe he wouldn't. The marriage wouldn't be valid, wouldn't be legal, even if he did."

Elizabeth turned away, frustrated. What Malachi said was true. Breaking the law by harboring fugitive slaves was one thing. Papa would be in trouble only if he got caught, and he wasn't going to get caught. But what good would performing an illegal marriage make? She and Malachi still wouldn't be able to live together as man and wife. She remembered the tales her mother told her, passed down from her Cherokee great-grandmother. Things were so much simpler then. All a man and woman had to do to become man and wife was perform a ritual dance at the time of the green corn festival, and they were wed.

"That's it!" She spun back to face Malachi. "I know what we'll do. We can perform our own marriage ceremony!"

Quickly she outlined all she knew about the green corn festival and the marriage dance. "I know it isn't a legal, valid marriage in the eyes of the law," she finished, "but it would be valid in the eyes of the God of my ancestors." She looked up at him, hopefully. "And it would protect Papa. He can't get in trouble for performing an illegal wedding ceremony if he doesn't know one took place."

Malachi sat back down on a rock, pulling her down beside him. He held her in his arms, silent for a moment, before quietly responding to her plan. "And you would be satisfied with such a marriage, Elizabeth? You would consider me your husband if we performed this green corn ritual?"

She nodded. "Would you consider me your wife?"

He smiled. "My great-grandmother lived free, in Africa. Marriages there were probably not a whole lot different from what you describe. I guess if the Gods of our ancestors approve, that should be good enough for we mortals. But what will we tell your mother and father?"

"We will tell them nothing, at least for now," Elizabeth said firmly. "You have your work to do, taking care of Flora and those who are undoubtedly getting ready to run as we speak. Papa is gone more than he's here, and Mamma is the only midwife for miles around, so she's gone a lot, too. Maybe we're wrong; maybe after the war it will be legal for us to wed. If so, we can have a regular ceremony. But if it still isn't legal, at least we won't have wasted all this time. We can explain then to Mamma and Papa. I'm sure they'll understand why we chose to do things this way."

Later that afternoon, under the pretext of harvesting blackberries, Elizabeth and Malachi slipped off into the forest together. They walked in silence, following the creek, until they came to a small grotto where lichen-covered granite boulders reached their strong shoulders toward the sky. A large flat rock with a pool of water in a bowl worried out of the granite over the millennia beckoned them forward.

"It's like an altar," Elizabeth whispered.

"This is where Jeremiah and I usually meet up, when he's bringing someone to me," Malachi said. "It's off the trail to your cabin, but you can't see in here from the creek, either, so it's safe."

"It's a beautiful spot," Elizabeth agreed, suddenly feeling shy. "I can't believe I haven't noticed it before—it's a perfect place for us."

With no one to witness their vows except a solitary raven perched high in a tulip poplar, Elizabeth and Malachi exchanged marriage vows.

Malachi pulled a freshly-killed rabbit from the rucksack he carried. "Elizabeth, I give you this gift of meat as a symbol of my ability to care for you, to provide for you, as proof of my manhood. I give this to show I honor you."

Elizabeth took the proffered rabbit and placed it on the stone altar. She then took two ears of dried corn from her basket and handed them to Malachi. "Malachi, I give you this gift of corn, a gift that represents Selu, the mother of corn. I give you this as a symbol of my ability to care for you, to provide for you, as proof of my womanhood. I give this to show I honor you."

Malachi took the corn and placed it next to the rabbit.

Elizabeth then pulled a jar of cornmeal from her basket, and sprinkled it over Malachi, then over herself. "As the corn takes root in our Mother the Earth, may our love also take root," she said.

Malachi wet his finger with water from the pool in the altar rock and streaked Elizabeth's forehead, then his own. "As the Gods of our ancestors blessed the corn with water and light so it might grow, may God so bless us now," he said.

Elizabeth took his left hand in hers. "Malachi, I take you as my husband."

Malachi let go of her hand, then took it back in his. "Elizabeth, I take you as my wife."

A cacophony of cawing from the raven in the tree made them both jump, then burst out laughing.

"Why do I think that raven just said, 'I now pronounce you husband and wife?'" Malachi said.

Elizabeth grinned. "Maybe he did. The raven was considered a sacred bird by my ancestors."

"So, is that how the marriage ceremony was done in the days of your great-grandmother?" he asked.

She shrugged. "I know the gifts of meat and corn were right, but aside from that, I have no idea. But it felt right to me. It *feels* right to me," she corrected herself.

"Me too," he said, as he took her in his arms and kissed her.

Chapter 8

It was Tuesday, and Tuesday was Cora's day for cleaning house. Dusting her furniture, cleaning the sinks and mirrors, and sweeping the hardwood floors were chores she did slowly, deliberately. These were times for reflection and contemplation, for descending into a meditative state. She remembered James-Cyrus saying how everything was sacred to her. He had been teasing, but she didn't mind because he had been right. Everything *was* sacred to her, including her house cleaning time.

Things would be so much easier for her if James-Cyrus wasn't such a skeptic. She knew powerful magic existed on Hoffmann Mountain because she had experienced it herself. She had spent the better part of the last forty years trying to understand its source, but while in many ways her skills were finely honed, that which she craved most desperately continued to elude her.

Her house in order, Cora pulled out a basket of wool and dragged her spinning wheel over near the window, where she could look across the meadow to Hoffmann Mountain as she worked. The soothing action of the spinning wheel and the warmth generated by the wool sliding through her fingers always sent her into a dreamlike trance. It would help her figure out what to do next.

Working this particular wool would be bittersweet. She'd promised Samuel a new cardigan sweater from the soft black Merino wool, but she wouldn't be knitting that now. The thought made her ache.

She pumped the treadle, gave the wheel a slow push, and slowly began feeding the raw wool through her fingers.

Samuel had known about the mountain's magic. Cora never would forget the day he came dashing into her kitchen, shaking like a leaf, and babbling about ghosts in the cabin on the mountain.

Cora had poured a glass of bourbon to calm him down. "Sit," she'd ordered, pulling out a chair from the kitchen table. She'd started to pour herself a glass, then changed her mind. "Now, tell me exactly what happened. Slowly."

Samuel took a small sip from his glass. "It's still there. The cabin. It's still there, up the mountain. I found it."

Cora felt a hot flash of excitement and disbelief at Samuel's revelation. Changing her mind about the bourbon, she poured herself a glass before joining him at the table. "But neither one of us could find it when we looked for it before. You said it had been burned down when William and Catherine moved down here to the valley."

"It was. I mean, I thought it was. That's what my father always told me. But it's still there." His voice had dropped to a weak whisper. "It's there, Cora, and it's full of ghosts."

"You don't strike me as the kind of man that believes in ghosts, Samuel."

He downed the rest of the bourbon with one quick gulp, hands shaking so badly he missed the table when he went to set down the glass. It shattered into a thousand bright prisms on the floor.

"Leave it for now," Cora commanded, taking Samuel's hands in hers. "Tell me, Samuel. What happened?"

"I've been looking for it for a couple of years." Samuel spoke so softly Cora could barely hear him. "I wanted to find it, and today when I hiked up the mountain…"

Her spinning was working its magic. The friction of the wool running through her fingers began warming her hands, and the soothing hum of the spinning wheel sent her mind flying back through time almost thirty years, back to that day in the kitchen and Samuel's fantastic tale…

When Samuel Hoffmann had something weighing heavily on his mind, he took to the mountain. Dwarfed by the grandeur of the ancient forest, his problems faded from his mind as he walked among the trees and granite boulders sprouting from the loamy ground like Hades' fist thrust through the earth's crust in search of Persephone's hand.

The mountain had been owned by his family for nearly two hundred years, and except for the few trees needed to build the house and barn in the valley, the forest had not felt the destructive mauling of the logger's axe or chainsaw. Still, the forest had suffered: Specters of giant chestnuts felled by the blight scarred the mountain, their slowly rotting trunks a silent reminder that nature's David and Goliath had done battle, and just like in the Bible, David had won.

The past week had been both the most joyous and the most painful of his life. It was hard to believe just seven days earlier, his son and daughter-in-law had been alive, happily anticipating the birth of their child. But Eliza's labor had come on suddenly, too suddenly, and she bled to death before Zachariah could get her to the hospital. The baby survived, but Zachariah was so grief stricken over the loss of his wife he put a bullet through his head, leaving Samuel with not only the grief of losing his only child but also the responsibility of raising his grandson without the benefit of a mother's or even a grandmother's love and guidance. Zachariah's upbringing had been his mother's doing until the day she died soon after her son's fourteenth birthday, but by then Zachariah had reached a certain level of self-sufficiency. Samuel had taken him hunting, taught him to milk cows and castrate bulls. Men's work. He intended to put his all into raising little James-Cyrus, but he was more than a little terrified of what lay ahead of him.

Thank God for Cora, he thought. I couldn't do it without her.

He hiked steadily up the mountain, stopping after an hour to drink from the creek and to rest. Sitting with his back against a rock, he idly started pitching pebbles into the water, trying to land one on a flat stone in the middle of the stream.

He almost pitched it before he realized what he held in his hand. A fairy stone, large in size and perfectly formed. "Well, I'll be hog tied," he said, startling himself with his own voice. "A fairy stone. How in tarnations did this get here?"

He turned the stone over in his hand, admiring its smooth cold edges, surprised by the warmth it seemed to generate from its center. He'd never seen a fairy stone so perfectly formed, nor one so large.

He took another drink from the stream, pocketed the stone, and continued up the mountain.

"Well I'll be hog tied," he said for the second time in as many hours when at last he stumbled into the clearing. "What the…"

He'd about given up ever finding his great-grandfather's cabin, and if he did find it, he'd been expecting a crumbling stone foundation, and maybe the charred skeletal remains of an outbuilding or two. What he gazed at now was remarkably intact, and silently beckoning to him from the center of the clearing.

A cold sweat beaded on his forehead. The cabin had burned to the ground, he'd been told; intentionally set on fire by his grandfather after the war's end to erase all traces of its ties to the underground railroad. Burned to keep their family secret from the vengeful, prying eyes of their neighbors who were not sympathetic to the plight of the slaves.

But here he stood, and there the cabin stood. Why had his grandfather lied about burning it down?

Heart beating wildly, he crept to the stone stairs leading to the front door, aware of his fear, annoyed by its presence. Three steps and he was at the door, hand on the latch. Shoulder against wood, the door only slightly protested before swinging open and into the room.

Samuel stood outside the open doorway, frozen, staring at the people bustling around the room. He recognized every one of them from the framed oil painting that had hung in the parlor since before he could remember. His great-grandfather William, a young man once again, and his first wife, Corrine. His grandfather, Cyrus, a young lad of maybe seven or eight, giving a little girl a piggy back ride and screaming an Indian war whoop as he bounced around the table.

Corrine looked up from her needlework, and Samuel found himself looking her square in the eye. "Close the door, won't you please, William? It's blown open again."

William set down the Bible he had been reading and rose from his chair. "That's the third time today," he said as his long strides brought him within an arm's length of Samuel. "I really must level it this afternoon."

Samuel heard the sound of the door slamming shut as he turned and ran.

The woolen yarn Cora was spinning broke, snapping her out of her trance. Her neck was taut, and she sat quietly rubbing out the kinks while she let her mind come fully back into the present.

She'd asked Samuel about the fairy stone, but when he reached into his pocket, the stone was gone, lost through a tear in the seam. She'd begged him to search for it, but his experience at the cabin had terrified him, and he'd refused, afraid of encountering more ghosts in the woods. Eventually, she'd quit pressing him about it. Her own furtive attempts to find it had always been for naught, and she'd given up trying after a few years.

But now James-Cyrus had been to the cabin, and had seen what was inside. Unlike his grandfather, he'd actually gone inside, and experienced some sort of transformation as a result. But he'd said nothing about finding a fairy stone, and the unlikelihood of such a find would certainly have prompted him to tell her if he had stumbled across it somewhere.

She gathered up her spinning supplies and put them away, then wandered out onto the front porch. The sun was sinking low over the mountains, and the deer were silently gliding into her meadow from the woods beyond to graze. An Io moth fluttered around her head, dancing on the soft breeze, then settled gently on the back of her hand. Slowly, Cora lifted the delicate creature until she was looking straight into its hematite eyes. The moth waved its antennae as if in greeting.

"He must have found my fairy stone," she whispered to the moth. "It has to be the same one I lost, and Samuel after me. It's the only explanation. It has to be."

It was time. James-Cyrus had to know the truth. Time was running out. Visions of Elizabeth were fading; a persistent ring of charcoal black expanded persistently toward images of her daughter every time she looked in the cauldron. Someone had to do something, and quickly, and James-Cyrus was the only one who possibly could do it.

She wandered over to the ancient cauldron in her yard and looked down at the reflection of the raven-haired girl standing in a stone grotto, wrapped in the arms of her lover, kissing him deeply. A raven was perched in the treetops above the lovers, and Cora was so startled she jumped when the bird looked her squarely in the eye, then opened its beak as if to let out a warning cry before taking flight.

"It's time, Elizabeth," she whispered. "Grandmother was right. What was torn asunder must be reunited. Only then can this grave wrong be righted."

She turned back toward the house. "And may heaven help me if I'm wrong."

Chapter 9

For the third time in less than a week James-Cyrus prepared to hike up the mountain to the cabin. What he expected to find up the mountain, he wasn't sure. But he knew he wouldn't be able to concentrate on anything else today if he didn't go up and take one last look around.

This time, he remembered to grab his bear bells from his top dresser drawer before going downstairs. His grandfather had given them to him as a gift before his first solo hike on the Appalachian Trail when he was eighteen. They weren't much to look at—just a couple of cheap Christmas sleigh bells, strung on a leather cord he could wear around his neck—but they made a cheerful, pleasant jingle when he hiked. Most importantly, he'd never surprised a bear when he was wearing them. After his experience with the mother bear yesterday, he didn't intend ever to surprise a bear again.

The sun was streaming through the parlor window, cradling his coffee table in the soft, warm glow of early morning, illuminating the fairy stone like a spotlight. Fairy stones were supposed to bring good luck, he'd read. Impulsively, he grabbed the stone and stuffed it in his pocket.

He thought about his most recent dream as he walked. In his dream, when he'd been sitting on the ladder inside the cabin, watching William, Catherine, and Elizabeth tend to the injured man—a runaway slave, James-Cyrus supposed—he'd been certain Elizabeth had seen him. She'd looked him right in the eye, and there had been recognition, he was certain of it. Still, he'd always believed dreams were tricks your mind played on you. Just because she'd seen him in his dream didn't mean she existed.

Two hours later, he stood breathless at the edge of the clearing. He'd made record time climbing the mountain, not even bothering to stop at the stream to share his snack with the ground squirrel.

He crossed the yard to the cabin and slowly climbed the stone steps, bracing himself for whatever he found. Grasping the latch, he pushed the door open.

She was there.

Elizabeth closed the book she was reading and stared at the man standing in her front door. She wasn't frightened, for how could she be afraid of a vision?

"Cyrus?" she asked softly, rising from her chair. The man did not reply.

"You aren't Cyrus, are you."

"No." The man's voice was hoarse, and Elizabeth could see he was trembling. *He doesn't understand what is* going on any more than I do, she realized. She also realized she wasn't afraid. "Come in. Sit down," she urged.

The man slowly walked into the cabin, scanning the room before letting his eyes rest on Elizabeth. "You're...Elizabeth?"

She nodded. "I seem to be at a disadvantage here. You know my name, but I don't know yours, sir."

"James-Cyrus." He cleared his throat. "James-Cyrus Hoffmann," he said, clearly this time.

Elizabeth blanched. "My name is Hoffmann. And my brother—his name is Cyrus James. You look just like him." She scrutinized his face a few moments. "Only, you look a little older than he."

James-Cyrus took a few steps toward the table. "I'm feeling a little shaky; may I sit down?" He sank into a chair before Elizabeth could reply.

"Would you like some water?" she asked. The man didn't look well, although, she had to admit, he looked considerably better than he did the last time he visited her. She was certain this was the same visitor she'd had before. "Or, maybe a cup of tea? I have some chamomile brewed."

He smiled weakly. "Tea would be great."

She poured him a cup, then sat down at the table across from him. "Where are you from? And what brings you all the way up here? We don't get many visitors."

"Thanks." He took a sip of his tea. "I came to see you."

"Do we know each other?"

"We only met the other day. I apologize, by the way, for departing so abruptly. That was rather rude of me. I wasn't feeling…myself."

"That's what you said then, too." Wondering if he still wasn't feeling himself—he seemed to think it had been only several days, not months, since their last meeting—she got up from the table and, opening a glass-fronted cabinet in the corner of the room, pulled out a small framed daguerreotype. "This is my brother, Cyrus," she said, handing the picture to James-Cyrus.

He stared at the photo. "We do look alike," he agreed, handing it back to her.

"I've been thinking, since you were here before, that maybe we're cousins." She put the daguerreotype back in the cabinet. "I don't have any first cousins, but maybe a second cousin or something. The resemblance is just too great to be a coincidence."

"Maybe."

"And I was also thinking, maybe you're the key to a mystery in my family." Elizabeth was getting excited now. "My grandfather, Benjamin, came to Virginia from Germany back during the Revolution. He had a brother, Harry, that came, too. They didn't come voluntarily; they were Hessian soldiers. After the war, Grandfather got married and claimed the land on this mountain. They chose to live up here because some of the people in the valley didn't take kindly to her being part Indian. He and my grandmother built this house with their own hands, but his brother and his wife decided to go farther south, to settle in North Carolina."

She paused a moment to take a drink of tea. "They never made it. My grandparents never heard from them again. Grandfather took off looking for them, but all he ever found was a broken wagon wheel. Most people assumed they were killed by Indians, although my grandmother never believed it. I wonder if you..."

"My grandfather's name was Samuel, not Harry," James-Cyrus said quietly. "He died only a few weeks ago."

"Oh!" Elizabeth's face fell. "Well...I'm sorry. Were you close to your grandfather?"

"He raised me. My parents both died when I was a baby."

"Oh! I'm sorry," she said again, blushing. She hadn't meant to be intrusive with the stranger. He looked so much like Cyrus she'd forgotten for a moment that he *was* a stranger.

James-Cyrus shrugged. "I guess you don't miss what you never had. Granddaddy was a great parent. I never felt unloved or unwanted. Plus, we have Cora down the road, and she sort of stepped in as my surrogate mother."

Elizabeth nodded knowingly. "My mother isn't really my mother. She's my aunt. I lost my mother when I was a baby, too. Papa married her sister." Elizabeth squirmed. She wasn't supposed to talk about this, she knew. Thankfully, James-Cyrus didn't press her on the matter.

He looked around the cabin. "Where are they now? Your parents, I mean."

"Mamma left this morning to go across the mountain. There's a little settlement there, and two of the womenfolk were due to deliver babies this week. Mamma's a midwife," she added hastily, seeing the look of confusion on the visitor's face.

"Papa's a circuit rider, although recently he's been riding along with General Sheridan's troops. I'm worried sick about him," she confided. "Cyrus fights for the Yankees—he's up in Pennsylvania someplace right now—but Papa says the southern troops need spiritual guidance as much or more than the Yankees, so that's where he is."

"So you're alone here? Is that safe?"

"Not alone. Malachi's here." She paled. *How could I mention Malachi to this stranger?*

"Who's Malachi?"

"My—" she stopped herself. She'd almost slipped and said 'husband.' "A family friend."

What was it about this stranger that made her forget herself; made her say things she was careful not even to say in front of Mamma? Malachi was in the barn making plans for getting the fugitive hiding there to the next safe house. She hoped he would take his time, but even as the hope flashed through her mind, she heard the back door to the cabin open. In walked Malachi.

"It's all settled; we're leaving tonight," she heard him call from the kitchen. "We'll leave as soon as the moon..."

He did not finish his sentence. Standing in the doorway between the kitchen and front room, Malachi stared at the stranger in uniform drinking tea with Elizabeth.

"It's all right, Malachi," she said, rising quickly and, taking his arm, guiding him into the living room. "He's family. At least, we think…Malachi, this is James-Cyrus. James-Cyrus, this is Malachi."

James-Cyrus rose and extended his hand. "Pleased to meet you."

Malachi hesitated only a moment, then shook James-Cyrus's hand. "The pleasure is mine." He gave Elizabeth a questioning look. "This is your brother?"

She shook her head. "No, but the resemblance is strong, isn't it? And his last name is Hoffmann. It can't be a coincidence. We must be kinfolk."

The three sat back down at the table, the uncomfortable silence thick as the smoke from a green wood fire. Elizabeth felt compelled to break the silence, but was at a loss for words.

It was Malachi who finally spoke. Are you on leave?"

James-Cyrus looked momentarily confused. "Oh! The uniform. I forgot…yeah, I'm on leave." He squirmed in his seat, looking mighty uncomfortable, and for a fleeting moment Elizabeth wondered if he had abandoned his regiment.

Malachi pressed further. "What regiment are you with?"

Now James-Cyrus looked truly panic stricken. Elizabeth felt sorry for the stranger who felt to her like family. "Malachi, I don't think…"

"No, it's a fair question," James-Cyrus said. "The truth is, I'm not a soldier; I'm a cattle farmer. I don't know what I'm doing here or how I got here. I just—"

Before he could finish his sentence, Malachi jumped to his feet and grabbed the rifle in the corner, aiming it squarely at James-Cyrus chest. "Who are you? What are you doing here?" he demanded.

Elizabeth gazed steadily at Malachi. "Put the gun down, Malachi. He's not going to hurt us."

Malachi laughed, a daggered laughter that made her fearful for the first time since she'd known him.

"You are too trusting, Elizabeth. Just because he looks like your brother and says he shares your name doesn't make him someone we can trust. He's compromised this place. You're not safe, I'm not safe, no one is safe here anymore."

"You have nothing to fear from me. I have nothing to gain from compromising a safehouse," James-Cyrus said quietly. "You must believe me. What Elizabeth says is true. We are kinfolk, but if I told you exactly how, you'd never believe me."

"I'm listening." Malachi kept the gun aimed at James-Cyrus.

"I...I'm not from here," James-Cyrus began, the wild look in his eye betraying the calm demeanor of his voice. "I hiked up here a few days ago, came in the cabin, and here Elizabeth was. I came back a few days later and found nothing but an abandoned, crumbling building. Then today, here she was again."

Malachi cocked the rifle. "Outside. Now. Move! Elizabeth, you get to the barn as fast as you can. Stay low!"

Panic-stricken, Elizabeth stepped between Malachi and James-Cyrus. "What are you going to do, Malachi? He won't hurt us. I know it; I *feel* it."

"He's compromised us. Don't you understand? There are probably more of them out in the woods, just waiting for me to come out."

"It's all right," James-Cyrus said quietly. "I'll go. But believe me, your story is safe with me." With Malachi following close behind, he stepped to the front door and opened it before turning back toward Elizabeth. "I'm not a bounty hunter. No one followed me. No one could."

With that, he stepped through the front door and disappeared in a flash of light.

Malachi jumped back, pulling Elizabeth to the floor and throwing his body across hers as if to protect her from the flash, but it took only moments to realize there was no sound of gunfire; that no enemy bounty hunters had fired at them from the door.

He helped her back to her feet. Cautiously, they walked hand in hand to the door and out into the front yard.

Malachi turned to her and frowned. "Where did he go?"

The sun was just beginning to set over the misty mountain when James-Cyrus arrived at Cora's. He'd ridden Chance, and he quickly turned her out into the sheep pasture before heading into the house. He was eager to tell Cora what had happened at the cabin.

He found her in the kitchen. She'd just poured herself a cup of tea and was slathering fresh-churned butter on a thick slab of toasted seed bread.

"You look like you need something stronger than tea," she said, reaching for the whiskey she kept in the cupboard. "Would you like toast, too?"

"Please." He was used to Cora's odd mixture of food and beverage; having toast and whiskey for dinner seemed perfectly natural at her house.

She buttered a second slab of toast for him and handed it to him perched on top of his whiskey glass, then picked up her own food and tea. "Come. Walk with me out to the yard."

As they walked, he told her all he could remember about his encounter with Elizabeth and Malachi. Cora chuckled. "Malachi was a runaway slave. He worked as a shepherd, there to escort fugitives between safe houses. He was afraid you'd ratted them out. You're lucky he didn't shoot you then and there, right inside."

"That's a sobering thought. Although, I guess he couldn't really have killed me, since I hadn't been born yet." He paused. "Why do I get the feeling none of this surprises you, Cora? How do you know that about Malachi? That he was a runaway slave and a shepherd?"

They'd stopped walking, and were standing in front of the cauldron. "Do you remember my telling you that the universe is a magical and mystical place, James-Cyrus? To believe what your eyes were showing you and your heart was telling you, not what logic told you?"

"Of course I remember. You tell me that all the time. Only now," he teased, "I'm starting to believe it's true and that you aren't just a lovable but crazy old woman."

Cora ignored the ribbing. "Look. In the water. Tell me what you see."

He leaned over the cauldron. "I see my reflection."

"Look closer. Not straight down, sort of look at an angle, across the water's surface."

He looked again, and what he saw almost made him drop his toast. "Elizabeth! Cora, that's her!"

Cora nodded.

"But how is it possible we're seeing her in the water?" He couldn't stop staring at her reflection. She was wearing the same dress she'd had on when he saw her that day, and was peering out the window of the cabin. She looked like she was crying. "She looks so sad," he said.

"She looks that way often these days," Cora said as they turned and walked back to the house. "Come up on the porch. I need to tell you a few things about the Hoffmann family."

"Granddaddy was always vague about family matters." James-Cyrus sank into one of the rocking chairs on the porch. "Other than what happened to my parents when I was born, I don't know much of anything. I see the names on the gravestones in the family cemetery. Other than what I've gleaned from them, the family history is one big mystery."

"Not a mystery, James-Cyrus. Not to me, anyway. And not to your grandfather. But it was more than he could absorb—Samuel wasn't able to let go of the logical and believe in the magical. It frightened him, so he tried to shield you from it."

"Shield me from what? Cora, what's the big mystery? What is going on around here?"

Cora set her tea cup on the wicker table between the rocking chairs. I'm going to tell you, but first you tell me this. Did you have anything unusual in your pocket? Something you found recently?"

He pulled his fairy stone from his pocket and set it in her outstretched hand. "How did you know?"

She didn't answer immediately, but cradled the stone carefully in the cup of her hand. After a moment, she handed it back. "Do you feel the warmth it generates?"

"It isn't cool to the touch, like most stones," he agreed. "But what does this have to do—"

"I'm getting to that," she said, and reached over to take James-Cyrus' hand. "It started back in 1966, on the day your grandfather and I first met...

Chapter 10

1966

By his own admission, Samuel Hoffmann wasn't much of a hunter. It wasn't that he had some moral objection to killing animals for food—after all, he raised the finest Angus beef in Virginia. But his eyesight wasn't perfect, and his aim was poor. He was always afraid he'd wound an animal rather than kill it, a thought that more often than not kept him from pulling the trigger on his rifle.

That he had no intention of shooting a deer didn't keep him from grabbing his rifle and taking to the woods. Before his wife's death, he felt less guilty about wandering off and ignoring farm chores if he told her he was going hunting. She never complained when he came home empty-handed. But she was gone now. So, too, was Zachariah, off to study veterinary medicine at Virginia Tech in Blacksburg. Samuel hoped it would keep him from being drafted. Too many boys were dying in Viet Nam as it was. He had no intention of letting his only child die fighting someone else's war.

He'd spoken with his son earlier in the day, when Zachariah called to tell Samuel he wasn't coming home for the summer as they had planned. "I met someone, Dad," he'd said, and Samuel could hear the grin in his voice through the telephone lines. "I can't come home, or someone else will sweep her off her feet."

Samuel had been disappointed, but he understood. Still, Zachariah's unexpected decision gave him reason enough to take the day off and go hunting. It wasn't deer season, but he never left his own property, and since he didn't intend to shoot anything anyway, what difference did it make?

So there he was, roaming the forest, following the animal trails that crisscrossed the mountainside like a giant checkerboard. Somewhere high up the mountain, he knew, were the ruins of his great-grandfather's cabin. He always thought he might accidentally stumble across the place, but his own father had been vague about its exact location on the mountain, and Samuel had never felt compelled to instigate a methodical search. There probably wasn't much left of the place at this point in history, other than perhaps a crumbling stone foundation that was probably so overrun with ivy he'd not see it anyway.

He'd been walking an hour when he heard a rumble of thunder drift over the mountain. He thought of turning back, but he was thirsty, and the creek was only a few hundred yards ahead. He'd get a drink first, then turn toward home. Chances were as good as not that the storm would never reach this side of the mountain, but there was no point in tempting fate.

When he reached the water, he flopped down on his stomach and drank deeply. The water was cold and had a vaguely mineral taste. It was the best water on earth, as far as Samuel was concerned, although recently he'd read the mountain streams were becoming contaminated and were unfit to drink. He'd never gotten sick though, and until he did, the pleasure of drinking mountain spring water was a vice he intended to keep.

His thirst slaked, Samuel turned to retrace his steps down the mountain.

And then he saw her: a young woman perhaps twenty-five years in age, slumped against a rock ten feet further up the creek. She was barefoot, her long, calico dress torn and grass stained. "Miss?" he called, scurrying over the rocks to where she lay. "Miss?"

The woman's eyes fluttered slightly, and she mumbled something Samuel could not understand.

"Miss, wake up!" Samuel placed his hand on her shoulder, shaking her gently. "Are you hurt?"

Her eyes opened again. "My ankle. I hurt my ankle."

Samuel looked at the woman's ankle and let out a long whistle. "You sure did mess that up but good," he agreed. "What are you doing, wandering alone out here in the mountains all by yourself?"

"William," she whispered. "William." A look of panic flooded her pale face as she struggled to get up.

"It's all right," he soothed. "William's not here. I'm Samuel, Samuel Hoffmann, and I'm going to help you, okay?"

"I have to find William," she said weakly. "I have to find my children."

"I'll help you find your family," Samuel promised, "but first we have to get you off this mountain. Can you stand on your own?"

She nodded, and Samuel helped her to her feet. Her bad ankle, however, refused to support her weight, and Samuel suspected she would have collapsed like a rag doll had he not held her up.

"What's your name, miss?" he asked. The woman looked too young to be called ma'am, despite her assertion she had a husband and children somewhere.

"Cor…" the woman struggled. "Cor…"

"Cora? All right then, Cora, you just lean on me," he said, guiding her left arm around his neck and putting his own arm around her waist. Her skin was hot to the touch; she was burning up with fever. "We'll take it slow."

It was hard work, for he had to more or less carry the sick and injured stranger down the mountain. He quickly abandoned his rifle; he could come back for it later. He prayed they made it back to the valley before the storm hit or darkness fell; he wasn't sure he'd be able to follow the deer trail once the daylight failed.

Three hours later, an exhausted Samuel collapsed onto his living room couch. Somehow he'd managed to get Cora down the mountain—thank heavens, the thunder he'd heard never did amount to anything—up the front porch stairs, and into the downstairs guest room without further injury to her swollen ankle. He'd coaxed a bowl of chicken noodle soup and a couple of aspirin down her throat, then tucked her into the bed with an ice pack on her ankle.

He needed a whiskey. He wasn't much of a drinker, but he kept a bottle of Johnny Walker Red in the kitchen cabinet. Now seemed an appropriate time to have a shot. He needed to figure out what to do.

He hauled himself off the couch and wandered into the kitchen to look for the scotch. He tossed a handful of ice into a tumbler before pouring a couple splashes of the amber liquid over top.

He'd called the local sheriff and state police, inquiring whether anyone had filed a missing person's report for someone matching Cora's description or for a married couple named Cora and William. When he got negative responses, he quickly hung up before they could ask too many questions.

He sipped his scotch, savoring the burn as it trickled down his throat.

Cora's ankle was badly sprained, but he didn't think it was broken. He didn't think she could have put any weight on it at all if it had been broken. Still, it probably was a good idea to have the doctor stop by and take a look. He and Doc Aker had been buddies since high school. He'd pay a house call if Samuel asked him to.

The problem was, how did he explain to the doctor who Cora was? Finding a strange woman unconscious on the side of the mountain sounded absurd even to him. Then there was the way she was dressed, like an actress out of a movie about pioneer life. Women simply didn't go hiking barefoot through the mountains in long calico dresses. And if she really did have a husband and children, where were they? Were they lost up on the mountain, too?

He made himself a roast beef sandwich and took that and his drink back to the living room. The sandwich bread was a little stale, but he was so hungry he didn't care.

There was another thing troubling him, he realized. The woman looked familiar. She did not appear to recognize him, and he certainly couldn't think where he might have met her. To his recollection, he'd never known a woman named Cora before. He quickly ran through the names and faces of the women who had been friendly with his deceased wife. Nothing there rang a bell with him, and besides, she was too young to have been in his wife's social circle. Still, there was something about her that was as familiar to him as his own face.

He polished off his sandwich and scotch, cleaned up the dishes, then checked on the sleeping stranger in his guest room. He was fairly sure she'd sleep through the night. He'd make the decision about calling the doctor in the morning.

He closed the door gently and headed upstairs to bed.

She awakened the next morning to the sound of a wren fussing in the magnolia tree outside the bedroom window. Her ankle throbbed, but her head felt much better. She sat up in bed and surveyed her surroundings, her eyes gliding past the cane-backed rocking chair in the corner of the room before settling on a bureau beneath the window. Corrine let out a gasp.

Sitting on the bureau was a pale green bowl and water pitcher. Purple irises circled the rim of the bowl, and a cluster of dogwood and redbud blossoms graced the front of the pitcher.

She crept out of bed and hobbled over to the bureau. It was her bowl and pitcher set, she was certain of it. Trembling, she lifted the pitcher and turned it over. *EMH, April 4, 1842.* Ester Mae Hoffmann, William's sister. She'd painted the set for them as a wedding present.

"It was my great-grandmother's," Samuel said. She'd been so absorbed in studying the pitcher she hadn't heard him come into the room. "It's one of the few heirlooms I have that hasn't been broken or lost over the years."

What do you mean it was your great-grandmother's? It's mine! she wanted to scream. Instead, she carefully set the pitcher back in the bowl. "It's beautiful," she said.

Samuel nodded. "I reckon you'll be wanting to wash up a bit. I'll show you where the bathroom is."

He held her arm and helped her down the hall, stopping outside a half-open white door. "Here you go," he said.

"Inside?" Corrine was aghast.

Samuel arched one eyebrow. "The house is old, but we do have indoor plumbing. See?" He stepped into the room, and turned a knob on a white basin. "Running water." His hand pushed down on a shiny lever on a strange contraption next to the sink, and with a loud *whoosh*, the water in it's low bowl disappeared into the floor. "Flush toilet. All the comforts of home."

She gasped. *Where did the water go?* she wanted to ask. She held her tongue. Samuel seemed to think these strange-looking furnishings should be familiar to her. She didn't want to do anything that betrayed that notion, not until she figured out what had happened to her. Instead, she said nothing.

"I've put towels and soap out for you. I also took the liberty of putting some of my wife's old clothes in there, in case you'd be wanting to change out of that dress." He smiled grimly. "Never quite knew why I held on to so many of her things after she died. Guess now it's a good thing that I did."

"Thank you," she said, looking down at her torn and stained dress. "Fresh clothing will feel nice."

Samuel nodded, and exited the...what had he called it? The bathroom. She shut the door behind him, and slowly began to undress.

She tentatively turned a knob on the large white washtub next to the toilet. Warm water gushed out, disappearing down a hole in the tub. A stopper rested on the tub's edge; she plugged the hole. When it was half full, she turned off the water and eased her aching body into the blissfully warm water.

There were too many questions. The Grandmother had taught her the universe was full of magic, and she was well-versed in the magical healing properties of herbs. But this was an altogether different sort of magic, some sort of spell the universe had cast over her. 'Believe what you see,' the Grandmother had said when she appeared to Corrine...was it only yesterday? The Grandmother knew what had happened, of that Corrine was certain.

What was torn asunder must be reunited; only then can this grave wrong be righted. Somehow, she would be reunited with her family. That had to be what the Grandmother meant.

Samuel Hoffmann. Was it a coincidence they shared a surname? He said his bowl and pitcher set belonged to his great-grandmother, but they were hers, or at least, they had been, and she was nearly half his age. Her children were babies.

He called her Cora. Cora she would remain until she unraveled the mystery of what happened to her. Samuel bore a striking resemblance to William. They were kin, she felt it in her heart. She would be safe here.

Feeling refreshed, Cora exited the bathroom and went in search of Samuel. It felt funny, wearing trousers like a man, yet oddly freeing, too. Skirts could be so cumbersome, getting twisted around her ankles and tripping her up at the most inopportune times. She once spilled a whole bucket of wild huckleberries because she tripped over a tree root and got her feet entangled in her skirts.

She found Samuel in the kitchen. He looked up and smiled. "You look better. Not limping nearly so much now."

"I feel much better, thank you. Not nearly so much pain. The bath was wonderful."

Samuel opened a door to a large white cabinet, and she felt a blast of icy air from inside. "I was just going to fix myself a sandwich. Would you like one? You must be hungry."

"I am," she admitted. "Whatever you're having is fine."

She watched in rapt fascination as Samuel pulled jars of pickles, a creamy white sauce, and thin slices of meat from the white box. He opened a drawer and retrieved a head of crispy lettuce. She was dying to ask questions, but she'd felt foolish enough being so surprised at the bathroom. She suspected Samuel would think her daft if she asked more questions about things he clearly took for granted.

"Doctor Pepper or Coke?" he asked.

A wave of confusion swept across her. "Neither, thank you. My ankle is fine; I don't think I'll be needing a doctor."

Samuel gave her an odd smile. "I'm having Doctor Pepper," he said, pulling two glass bottles from the cold cabinet and opening them. "Here, you have one, too."

She waited to follow his lead, and when he drank, she drank deeply, too. Her mouth filled with icy cold foam that bubbled up into her nose. Feeling herself choke, she tried to cover her mouth and nose with her hand, but it was too late—she sprayed the mouthful of bubbling liquid across the kitchen.

So much for not looking daft. "Oh! I'm so sorry!" Embarrassed, she picked up a rag from the counter and started mopping up the mess.

"No, don't worry about it—I should have warned you it was fizzy," Samuel said, taking another rag and easing himself down on his knees to help her. "There, see? Nothing to be embarrassed about."

"Things are just so different here…" She thought about William, who looked so much like Samuel; and about Cyrus and baby Elizabeth. *Elizabeth.* She braced herself for the inevitable flow of milk that came when she thought of her daughter. To her surprise and sorrow, her breasts remained dry, but her eyes filled with tears.

"Here now, sit down and eat," Samuel said, pulling out a chair for her and setting her sandwich and Doctor Pepper in front of her. "I never knew a problem that didn't look a whole lot better on a full stomach."

After lunch, Samuel headed out to the barn to meet the veterinarian, who was coming to check on a calf with a lame leg. Cora picked up what was left of her Doctor Pepper and wandered toward the parlor. Samuel hadn't called it that; he'd called it a living room. She quickly ran through the list of new names she'd acquired that day: bathroom, refrigerator, soda pop, living room. She wasn't sure which of the new experiences she liked best—the bathroom, with its warm water and flush latrine (she'd forgotten the word Samuel had used for it, and had been to embarrassed to ask him again), or the soda pop. After her initial shock of finding her mouth and nose full of frigid foam, she discovered it was delightfully sweet and thirst quenching. Next time, she'd ask for the Doctor Coke instead of the Doctor Pepper. It probably tasted different, she reasoned, or Samuel wouldn't have offered her both kinds.

The living room was comfortably furnished, with an enormous billowy sofa and two arm chairs. A large window overlooked the front porch and yard. The wall opposite the window was nothing but bookcases, filled with books. Books! At least she'd have something to do until she figured out what had happened to her.

She browsed through the titles, but few were familiar to her. There was a Bible, and the Complete Works of Shakespeare, but also authors named Hemmingway and Faulkner. There were even books that were written by women—Edith Wharton, Eudora Welty, Flannery O'Connor. Curious, she selected a book, *My Antonia*, by a woman author named Willa Cather and headed for the sofa to curl up and read.

The framed portraits on the wall above the sofa caught her attention before she could sit down. Tears filled her eyes again. The picture in the middle was a painting of William, Cyrus, and herself. Esther Mae had painted it when she visited them a few months before Elizabeth was born.

She examined the portrait more closely. This wasn't the original picture, she realized, but some kind of quality reproduction of the original. Her cheeks had been given some sort of rosy blush she didn't remember, and much of the background had been cut out of the picture. She liked this one better, she realized.

Struggling to control her emotions, she wiped away a stubborn tear that refused to stay contained as she examined the smaller pictures hanging on either side of the painting. The one on the left was of a young man who looked exactly how she imagined Cyrus would look when he was older. The man in the picture looked twenty-two or twenty-three, perhaps, and was wearing some sort of military uniform.

It was the picture to the right of the family portrait, however, that at last made her break down completely. It was of an older couple, perhaps in their sixties, leaning on the railing of a what she guessed was some kind of fancy boat, and waving. The man had a trim beard and spectacles; the woman gray-streaked hair tucked tidily into a dramatic feathered hat. Despite their ages, she had no doubt who they were.

"It's not possible," she sobbed. "It can't be William and Catherine. It can't be."

Cora barely heard Samuel come back in the house. Her tears had subsided, replaced with a dull ache in her heart and numbness everywhere else that she hoped would never go away.

"That's my great-grandfather William and great-grandmother Corrine," he said, gesturing toward the portrait. "The little guy is my grandfather Cyrus." He pointed to the picture of the young man in uniform. "That's Cyrus, too. He fought in the Union army during the Civil War. Brave thing to do, being a Virginian and all."

Cora nodded mutely. She had no idea what he was talking about.

"Down here," Samuel moved to the picture to the right, "is William again, with his second wife, Catherine."

"What happened to her?" Cora could barely get the words out. "What happened to Corrine?"

"No one seems to know," Samuel said. "It happened well over one hundred years ago. My grandfather was three at the time, and until the day he died he insisted his mother stepped out the front door and vanished into thin air."

"He saw what happened?"

Samuel scratched at his chin whiskers. "Well, he was only three. Three-year-olds can have mighty vivid imaginations." He chuckled. "When my boy Zachariah was three, he used to insist one of our more cantankerous bulls was really a dinosaur that was terrorizing the entire Shenandoah Valley at night. You know little boys and dinosaurs."

She didn't, but chose not to tell Samuel so.

"Still, Granddaddy Cyrus was always insistent that what he saw was real. Corrine was there one instant and gone the next." He leaned in toward the picture, then frowned. He turned toward Cora. "You could be her twin."

"Look again, Samuel."

He studied the portrait. "Yup. We have to be kinfolk. This is unbelievable; how much you look like her."

"That portrait was painted by Esther Mae Hoffman, William's older sister," Cora said. She pointed to the rounded belly of the woman in the portrait. "She was seven months along. Catherine was a midwife and her sister, and she delivered the baby a few months later, a baby girl named Elizabeth." She struggled to keep from crying again.

"What happened to Corrine happened when the baby was only a few weeks old."

Samuel stared at her. "How do you know all that?"

"Wait here a moment." She ran down the hall to the bedroom, ignoring the occasional stabs of pain in her ankle, retrieved the dress she'd been wearing when Samuel found her, and ran back to the living room.

"Look." She held the dress up next to the portrait. "What do you see?"

This time it was Samuel's eyes that welled up with tears.

It didn't take Cora long to catch up on more than one hundred years of history. She read voraciously, especially books about the Civil War and underground railroad. She was proud of what her family had done: William and Catherine and Elizabeth running a safe house for fugitives, and Cyrus fighting for the North.

William and Catherine. She smiled at the thought. Both her husband and her children had been well cared for and loved after she disappeared. She still missed them all terribly. It was hard to believe they were all dead and buried. Samuel had shown her the small family cemetery in the pasture beyond the barn, at the base of the mountain. William, Catherine, and Cyrus had lived long and productive lives. They had been happy. For that she was grateful.

She wished she knew more about Elizabeth's life. Samuel said she'd moved west—Ohio, he thought—after the war ended, but he was vague with the details. She hoped her daughter had been happy.

They decided to tell people she was his second cousin from Ohio. She also decided to remain Cora. "Corrine died that day," she told him. "It will be much easier for me to start a new life if I have a new identity."

Samuel agreed. "It would be kind of difficult to explain to people why my great-grandmother is nearly half my age," he said dryly.

The decision to take the last name Spellmacher had begun as a joke. Samuel had teased her about her belief in the healing power of herbs, and her Indian beliefs about stones and trees having spirits. "Don't you do your spell making on me," he'd joked when she'd inquired if there were witch hazel, black cherry, and slippery elm trees nearby so she could brew up some of her remedies. "I'm liable to end up on the moon during the twenty-first century." She'd decided on the spot to take the name Spellmaker; Samuel suggested changing it slightly to Spellmacher, and the issue of her name was settled.

She'd cried when the issue of her living quarters were settled. Samuel presented her with the deed to the small sheep farm adjacent to his own property on her birthday, six weeks after she'd arrived.

"I'll repay you someday," she promised through her happy tears.

"Nonsense," he growled. "William was the one who originally bought that land. He gave it to my granddaddy Cyrus and my grandmother as a wedding present. It's only right it should be yours now. It's a small miracle my tenants wanted out of their lease so they could buy their own place up toward Bridgewater. Besides," he winked at her, "How many men get to give their great-grandmother a one-hundred-forty-fifth birthday present?"

"Very funny. Perhaps we should simply say twenty-fifth birthday and keep it at that." She hugged him. "But I do thank you, Samuel. You've been a dear."

She found her cast iron cauldron tucked away in a sheep pen in the small barn a week after moving into her new home. "I can't believe they brought this down from the mountain!" she told Samuel when he stopped by later that day. "It must weigh at least hundred pounds."

"I'd forgotten about this old thing," he said. "It's been here as long as I can remember; I know both my grandmother and my mother used to make apple butter in it." He peered inside. "It's not in very good condition. Rusty. Want me to help you clean it up?"

"No, I'll enjoy doing it," she said.

She wiped all the cobwebs from the cauldron, then oiled it until it gleamed. Samuel fashioned a sturdy tripod so Cora could hang it over a fire in her yard.

"It's like trying to move a whale across dry land," he grumbled as they struggled to roll the behemoth to the place she'd selected in her yard. "One of the great inventions of the last hundred years was the modern stove. You really ought to give yours a chance."

"I will," she promised. "I got used to using the one at your house. But this is like having an old friend here with me." She patted the cauldron with affection. "It reminds me of home." She turned away, both to turn on the water and run a hose into the cauldron to fill it, and because she didn't want Samuel to see her eyes tear up. Thoughts of the cabin on the mountain still caused her pain so exquisite she could hardly breathe. "Do you think we'll ever figure out what happened to me, Samuel?"

He swatted at a mosquito buzzing near his ear. "I read a book about a year ago. *The Haunted Mesa*, it was called. Louis L'Amour. It's set out west, and it's about this guy who steps back and forth through these time warps—he called them windows in time, I think—back to the time of the ancient Anasazi Indians. Near as I can reckon, something like that must have happened to you. Only, the guy in the book could come and go. He knew how to do it. You said you don't know what caused your time jump."

"And you're sure the cabin is gone?"

He nodded. "Granddaddy—Cyrus—said it was burned after the war so no one could link the family to the underground railroad. I don't have any reason not to believe him. All these years hiking that mountain, I've never even found where it was."

"I looked, too," she admitted. "I've spent hours up there in the past few weeks. But everything looks so different. The stream doesn't even seem to follow the same course, and the trees aren't the same. It's as if I'm searching for my home on an entirely different mountain."

"I guess in a way you are." He gave Cora a squeeze and kissed her on the cheek. "I'm going home; I'll see you tomorrow or the next day."

Cora watched as he got in his truck and drove down the gravel drive that linked their two homes. Home. Would she ever feel that this little house was home? The cauldron gave her comfort, as did the copies of the pictures Samuel had given her of her family. But so much changed, she felt like she'd moved to a foreign land. The language was strange—she'd mastered 'refrigerator' and 'soda pop' quickly, but she'd never get used to calling a latrine anything other than a latrine, whether it was inside with a flushing handle or simply a hole in a shed outside.

The food, too, was strange. The bread Samuel bought at the store was as soft and white as a cloud on a summer day, but had none of the nutty, earthy taste of the breads she baked at home. Peaches out of a tin can tasted green. Her peaches had cinnamon and nutmeg and tasted like summer even in the middle of February.

She wasn't very impressed with what Samuel called 'modern medicine' either. She'd tasted a little of the thick brown liquid she'd found in a bottle labeled 'cough syrup' in Samuel's medicine cabinet. It had made her gag, then vomit. There was none of the soothing richness of her own black cherry cough remedy in the modern concoction. And while Samuel teased her about making what he called 'witch brews', he quit laughing when the salve she made from jewelweed took the itch out of the poison ivy rash he got clearing brush behind her barn, and when the nettle tea she concocted took the ache out of his stiff joints when his rheumatism flared up.

Not that she didn't like some of the things in her strange new world. She loved Doctor Pepper, washing machines, and being able to wear trousers. She didn't think she'd ever wear a dress again, in fact. Besides, the dresses women wore now were too short, tight, and uncomfortable looking. Trousers, especially blue jeans, were so much better.

So absorbed in her thoughts did she become she didn't realize her cauldron was full until water started pouring over the top. She threw the hose aside, then ran her hands over the top of the water, smoothing its ripples as if she were smoothing wrinkles from a piece of fabric. As she moved her hand along, a picture appeared on the surface of the water. She froze, staring at the picture, afraid one wrong movement would cause the image to melt into the black depths of the cauldron.

She could see the cabin, as clear as if she were standing in the clearing. The large hemlock stood protectively at the edge of the clearing while the roses look like they were dancing to the music of the mountain wind.

The roses weren't the only dancers Cora saw reflected in the water. Dancing around the cauldron, splashing playfully at the water, was a little girl of about four, with long dark curls and eyes that held too much wisdom for one so young.

"Elizabeth?" she whispered.

Perhaps this was what the Grandmother meant when she said what was torn asunder must be reunited. She, Corrine—Cora—would be given the opportunity to watch her daughter grow up after all, that the magic in the cauldron was the righting of the grave wrong of her being hurtled through time.

For the first time since Samuel found her on the mountain, the finality of her situation registered in her heart. She wasn't going back. She would not be physically reunited with her family. She hadn't realized how high her hopes had gotten these past few months. And yet, she didn't cry. Her tears had long ago been spent; the hole in her heart and her soul had been patched back together by the loving kindness and generosity Samuel showed her.

She looked back at the little girl in the cauldron. Her sister, Catherine, wandered into the picture, and Elizabeth jumped into her arms, hugging her fiercely. Cora smiled.

"Thank you, Catherine, for taking care of my baby," she whispered.

"And thank you, Grandmother." She bowed her head. "Thank you."

Chapter 11

James-Cyrus's whiskey was long gone, and he had forgotten the toast he held in his hand. What Cora was telling him was wild, too fantastic to be true, and for a few moments, he worried she had lost her mind.

But the more she spoke, the more he realized he believed her. It made so many things about his upbringing, things his grandfather had refused to discuss, make sense. He'd always wondered why Samuel had been so determined James-Cyrus not explore the mountain, and why he'd gotten so upset that day when he was ten and sneaked away and found the cabin. Was he afraid James-Cyrus would disappear into the same time warp that brought Cora to them?

"I don't think that was it," Cora said when he posed the question out loud. She briefly filled him in on what happened the day Samuel had found the cabin the week after James-Cyrus's birth.

"So Granddaddy thought he was seeing ghosts?" He took a sip at his whiskey glass before he realized it was empty. "No wonder he didn't want me up there as a kid. Would you like more tea?"

Cora nodded, and he took his glass and her cup into the kitchen to refill them.

A question occurred to him as he sat back down. "I don't understand something. Why didn't Granddaddy vault back? Why didn't he have the same thing happen to him that happens to me when I go up there?"

Cora shrugged. "I don't know. But the best guess I can make is while you actually stepped into the cabin, he stopped before crossing the threshold."

"Like he opened the window, but didn't go through it."

"If a window is what it is, then, yes."

"And you think the fairy stone is what opens it."

"It's the only explanation I can come up with. I found it just before I came here. I lost it along the way. Samuel found it, then lost it again. Now, you've found it, and you've been back and forth twice. It must be the stone."

He paused. "I went up another time. Between the two times when I saw Elizabeth. I didn't take the fairy stone with me, and when I got there, the cabin was crumbled and empty." He gave her an embarrassed grin. "I didn't tell you about that time, because I'd had a run-in with a she-bear and her cubs, and I knew you'd scold me for not wearing my bear bells."

"You're too old for me to scold. But that proves what we already suspected, doesn't it?"

They sat in silence, sipping their drinks and listening to a whippoorwill calling from the pasture. James-Cyrus wondered if Cora was thinking the same thing he was. He was afraid to ask.

As if reading his mind, Cora spoke. "I don't want to go back. Not anymore. You're my family now." She smiled, and reached across the wicker table to pat his hand.

"William and Catherine lived a happy life together. Cyrus turned into a fine man. I've gotten to see Elizabeth grow up by watching the water in the cauldron."

Her wrinkled face clouded. "I fear for Elizabeth, James-Cyrus. I have reason to suspect your granddaddy's story about her moving to Ohio wasn't true."

She set down her tea. "You asked how I knew about Malachi. I didn't, until recently. But I've been watching him and Elizabeth. They've fallen in love."

James-Cyrus looked skeptical. "Are you sure, Cora? Wouldn't that have been dangerous? A white woman falling in love with a…" His eyes widened. "That's why you're afraid."

She nodded. "I know I'm not wrong about this. A few days ago, I attended their wedding."

"You *what?*"

She filled him in on Elizabeth and Malachi's enactment of the green corn ceremony she'd witnessed in the cauldron. "There was no mistaking it. They were performing the ancient Cherokee wedding ceremony. They're married, at least, in their eyes."

James-Cyrus sat nursing his drink, looking deep in thought, as though trying to absorb what Cora was telling him. Finally, he spoke.

"I'm confused how you witnessed the marriage. I though you could only see Elizabeth when she was in the clearing, near the cauldron. I thought you said the cauldron was what allowed you to see her."

"It is. Or, at least, it was." Cora didn't blame James-Cyrus for sounding skeptical and confused. She was as confused as he was. "But that is exactly what makes me fearful. The magic seems to be spreading beyond the eyes of the cauldron. And there's more—a raven always is in the scene when I'm watching her. Now, our ancestors considered the raven to be a sacred bird, but in some traditions, the raven is an omen of death. That's what frightens me. And then there's the black ring. The images are always surrounded by a black ring, and it's getting bigger by the day. Pretty soon, I won't see anything at all."

They sat in silence, James-Cyrus finishing his scotch and Cora her tea. It was comforting having him sitting there next to her, Cora thought. Sitting there, listening, and *believing*. Samuel listened, but even after she made her leap to the future and convinced him she was Corrine, his great-grandmother; even after visiting the cabin and seeing through the window to the past with his own eyes, Samuel had never been a believer. He thought what had happened was some strange accident, a freak of nature, like the two-headed calf that had been born to one of his beef cows the year before James-Cyrus was born. Believing there was such a thing as magic upset his paradigm of what the universe was, and wasn't. That was why he sheltered James-Cyrus from the truth. But Samuel was gone now, and James-Cyrus was a grown man. He didn't need sheltering. He needed to know the truth.

He broke into her thoughts. "Did Granddaddy know about you seeing Elizabeth grow up by looking in the cauldron?"

Cora nodded. "I quit trying to show him after a few times. He never could see her, and he started becoming alarmed that I thought I could." She finished her tea and got up to stretch. "I think maybe the fact he never made the time leap prevented him from seeing her. Somehow, that must be what allows you and I to see her. I can't think of any other explanation."

"But you've been here for what, almost forty years? How come Elizabeth isn't forty when I see her, if she was only a few weeks old when you disappeared?"

Cora shrugged. "I don't know. But I've got a theory." The smile returned to her face. "Do you remember when you were a little boy, how it seemed forever between birthdays or Christmases? But now it seems like every time you turn around, the season has changed, or your birthday or Christmas has arrived. Time tends to speed up as we get older."

He gave her a quizzical look. "I don't understand what you're saying."

"I'm just suggesting maybe time appeared to go slower back then than it does now, so Elizabeth doesn't seem to be growing up as fast as you did, for example."

He nodded. "I guess that makes some sense." His head suddenly ached; this was all too much to absorb in one day. He stood up to leave. "I've got to go home. I'm exhausted. Can we talk more about this tomorrow?"

"Of course, love. I'll walk out with you to the pasture."

They were halfway down the stairs when another question popped into James-Cyrus's head. "How come my clothes change when I go back? Why do I end up wearing a Union soldier's uniform?"

"I've wondered that myself," Cora said, taking his arm as they strolled toward the pasture where Chance grazed peacefully among the sheep. "The only thing I can think is that because you look so much like Cyrus, whatever is causing this magic changes you into the uniform so Elizabeth won't be afraid of you. Men didn't wear shorts and tee-shirts back then. A man suddenly appearing in her house with his legs and arms uncovered would be a startling sight, to say the very least."

They said their good-byes, and James-Cyrus mounted Chance and trotted off toward home. Cora, his great-great—how many greats was it?—triple-great grandmother. It was too much. He'd wondered a few times as he grew up why the widowed Samuel hadn't married Cora, despite their age difference, when they obviously loved each other deeply. Their age difference. He laughed aloud. Here he'd always thought Granddaddy was so much older than Cora! Another family mystery solved, he thought.

After feeding the chickens and giving Chance a bag of oats and fresh bedding, James-Cyrus bounded into the house and up the stairs to the attic. He wasn't sure what he was looking for; he just felt that if he looked hard enough he'd find some clue to what happened to Elizabeth after she left Hoffmann Mountain.

He found it odd Samuel had told Cora Elizabeth had moved to Ohio. He didn't recall his grandfather ever speaking of relatives anywhere east of the Alleghenies. Did Samuel know for a fact Elizabeth had gone west, or did he make that story up so Cora would believe her daughter had lived a happy life? Had Samuel ever even talked to his grandfather Cyrus about what had happened to Elizabeth? James-Cyrus didn't think so. The family story was always that the cabin had been burned after the Civil War; that William and Catherine and Cyrus had moved down to the valley and built the house James-Cyrus now lived in. The house, the farm, had been handed down from one generation of Hoffmanns to the next ever since.

Cora deserved to know what had become of her daughter. He reached the top of the attic staircase and switched on the light.

The attic was filled with the musty memories of several generations of Hoffmanns. James-Cyrus pushed aside the trunks he knew contained his childhood memorabilia—everything from his Matchbox car collection to his original Star Wars action figures, Little League trophies, and souvenirs from childhood vacations with his grandfather to Niagara Falls, Yellowstone National Park, and Washington DC. He opened a dusty leather trunk he didn't remember seeing before. Inside, he found his mother's wedding dress, yellowed with age, and his parents' wedding picture.

He studied the photo. His mother, Eliza, had been so beautiful with her wild, unruly red curls and green eyes that, even on her wedding day, looked haunted, as though she knew tragedy lay ahead. Zachariah, his father, looked like a darker-haired version of James-Cyrus, and while he was sure he would have loved his father dearly had he survived, he never had quite gotten over feeling his father was weak, taking his own life when his newborn, motherless son needed him so desperately. Even though he knew it was unfair, he had always blamed his own failure at relationships on his father's loving his mother too much to go on without her. He desperately wanted a wife and children of his own, but here he was, in his early thirties, and he had never once had a relationship with a woman serious enough for him to consider proposing. The thought of loving—and losing—someone scared him too much.

He placed the photo back in the trunk and locked it. Pushing it aside, he opened several more trunks, finding moth-eaten baby clothes, chipped bits of china, and a mourning brooch apparently worn by his great-great-grandfather Cyrus's widow when he died.

He pocketed the mourning brooch, thinking Cora might like to have it. Finding nothing more of interest in the trunk, he reached up to shut the lid.

A slight shifting in the lid caused him to take a closer look. Feeling around inside the domed lid, James-Cyrus found a false ceiling, one that easily pulled away. Out tumbled a tatterworn book, its frayed, yellowing pages nearly unintelligible in the dim attic light.

He picked up the book, tipping its cover toward the light. *Cyrus James Hoffmann: An Accounting of My Life Thus Far.* His great-great grandfather's journal! Perhaps there was something in here that alluded to Elizabeth's fate.

He flipped off the light switch and headed downstairs to the living room. Tired as he was, sleep was the last thing on his mind.

He read well into the night, pausing only once to fix himself a sandwich and a cup of tea. He read with rapt fascination his great-great-grandfather's account of being a southerner and a Union soldier, of his close brush with death when a Rebel bullet went clear through his cap, grazing his skull and wounding him just badly enough he was granted a leave home to recuperate.

Taking the journal with him up to his bedroom, he crawled under the covers and continued reading of the joy and relief Cyrus's sister Elizabeth and mother Catherine displayed when he walked through the cabin door, injured but alive. James-Cyrus smiled; he could imagine Elizabeth throwing herself at Cyrus just as she had thrown herself at *him* when he first stumbled into the cabin.

His smile, however, was short-lived. He read on in horror as the events of the following days unfolded before him in his ancestor's shaky scrawl. He read on, until his eyes grew too heavy to keep open and the journal slipped from his hands.

James-Cyrus slept.

James-Cyrus was once again sitting in the hemlock tree at the edge of the clearing, peering down through the dusky twilight at the cabin below. A cool breeze foretold the coming of autumn as it gently rocked his perch, and he held on tightly so as not to fall. The forest was quiet save for the hypnotic gurgling of the creek as it danced down the side of the mountain and the far away mewling of a catbird.

The cabin door opened and Elizabeth slipped out into the growing darkness. She hurried across the clearing to the barn at the forest's edge, disappearing inside the structure only to emerge once again minutes later. Her eyes scanned the clearing's perimeter, pausing briefly as they rested on the hemlock tree. James-Cyrus shrank back, but she showed no sign of alarm. She beckoned, and the shadowy figures of two men—one the color of milky tea, one dark as the night itself—shrank into the gloomy clearing and stood at her side. James-Cyrus recognized the light-skinned man as Malachi.

The catbird drew closer, but the trio in the clearing paid it no heed. Instead, Malachi pulled the woman close and held her in his arms. The second man, by now an inchoate shadow in the darkening clearing, turned away, and suddenly James-Cyrus knew he was witnessing the exchange of a tender good-bye between lovers.

Mew, mew, quirt! The catbird was almost upon them. Fear. He could smell it, the putrid smell of grief, of death.

Stop! There is terrible danger here! He screamed with all his might, but Elizabeth and her companions did not hear. He scrambled down from the tree, breaking the last branch in his haste. He fell to the ground as the loud crackling of rifle fire burst through the night. The woman screamed as two grizzled men charged from the woods, shouting at the three to drop to the ground. The dark man fled toward the woods as yet another rifle burst ripped through the air. The man sagged to his knees, wavered a moment, then fell forward.

James-Cyrus tried to run to Elizabeth, but as fast as his feet moved, he covered no ground, running helplessly in place. Malachi pushed Elizabeth to her knees, shielding her from their attackers with his own sturdy frame. "Don't hurt her!" he shouted. "It's me you want. Don't shoot!"

The men raised their rifles, took aim, and shot. "Cyrus! Help us!" Elizabeth screamed as her protector crumbled to the ground.

James-Cyrus sat bolt upright in bed, awakened by his own scream.

Chapter 12

Elizabeth stepped out the back door of the cabin and breathed deeply. The scent of the mountains in spring always filled her with hope. It had been a hard winter, the weather alternating between gusty winds with freezing rain and snow, and a dry cold she could feel all the way to the most secret corners of her soul. While she and Catherine had stayed cozy in front of the hearth, knitting socks and quilting blankets, she was beginning to feel as though she would go mad if she didn't soon get her hands dirty in the cool soil of her garden.

Papa had gotten home right before Christmas, and stayed through mid-February before heading out on the circuit once again. While having him home for so long a spell was wonderful in many ways, it created problems for her and Malachi. Her husband—how she savored that word, *husband*—was with her so precious few days each month. Catherine was a sound sleeper. When only her mother was home, Elizabeth could sneak out of the cabin at night and join Malachi in the barn loft, sneaking back into the cabin before the sun rose in the morning. When Papa was home, she did not dare try to leave her loft bedroom.

Papa awakened at the sound of a mouse scurrying across the hearth.

But now, things were going to be different. They would have to be. She and Malachi had hoped to keep their vows secret until the war was over. That was no longer a possibility.

She sat in her mother's chair, enjoying the soft breeze wafting across the clearing and the warmth of the late afternoon sun as it began to slip behind the trees to the west. She rocked back and forth, humming a soft lullaby and cradling her arms as if holding a child. Malachi was expected home that night. She would tell him her news. Together, they would figure out the right way to break it to Catherine. She hoped her mother would understand.

Ultimately, though, she knew it didn't matter.

Her reverie was broken by the sound of a horse trotting up the path toward the cabin. Hastily, she slipped back inside and latched the door. She didn't want to be caught daydreaming on the back porch if the visitor wasn't friendly.

Catherine was in the front room, peering through the window curtain. "Mamma?" Elizabeth whispered as she crept into the front room. "Who is it?"

"I can't see yet," Catherine whispered. "Get the rifle, just in..." she let out a gasp. "Yes, I can! I can see!" She dropped the curtain and ran to the door, Elizabeth close behind.

Catherine threw open the front door. "Cyrus! You're home!"

Elizabeth slipped past her mother and dashed down the stone steps as her brother slid from his horse. "Cyrus!" She threw her arms around his neck, squeezing him so hard he let out a sharp yelp, causing her to jump back with alarm.

"I'm happy to see you too, little sister," Cyrus grinned. "You too, Mamma." He gave Catherine a squeeze. "But take it easy on this wounded soldier."

He removed his cap, revealing a bandage covering most of the top of his head. "It isn't as bad as it looks, really. Just bad enough to get me sent home for a spell." He grimaced. "Mostly, I have a raging headache. A week on the back of a horse didn't help that none, either. I'd kill for some willow bark tea."

Catherine reached up and gently fingered the bandage on her son's head. "What happened?"

"Got myself too close to a bullet." He untied his rucksack from the back of his horse. "It's just a graze wound, really. Let me put this old nag in the barn. Then I'll come inside and tell you everything."

While Catherine rummaged through the medicine cupboard for a fresh bandage and the witch hazel, Elizabeth bustled around the kitchen, fixing willow bark tea and slathering apple butter on a thick slab of cornbread for Cyrus. Her thoughts whorled through her head with the lightning speed of water tumbling over the rocks in the creek after a heavy storm. Cyrus, home! Her best friend and childhood playmate. The only person she'd ever told her every secret; that is, until Malachi.

They'd be the best of friends, she was sure, her brother and her husband. Cyrus would never question their motive for marrying in secret. Cyrus would never question Elizabeth's motives in anything, just as she would never question his. They loved each other, trusted each other, and supported each other, just as she and Malachi loved and trusted and supported each other.

She poured hot water from the kettle into two tea pots: chamomile for herself and her mother, willow bark to soothe her brother's aching head. His timing for coming home couldn't be better, she realized. Malachi was due that evening. She'd share her news with Cyrus first. Then when Malachi got home, she tell him, and together they'd tell Mamma. Having Cyrus behind them when they broke the news to Catherine would make it so much easier.

She finished the food preparations just as Cyrus came in from the barn. "Sit at the table here and let me re-bandage your wound while you eat," Catherine ordered.

Cyrus sank into a chair and allowed his mother to remove the bandage from his head.

"Why, it shaved your head clean right down the middle!" Catherine exclaimed. "I've never seen such a wound." She paled. "Cyrus, if you'd been an half an inch taller..."

"Or wearing my boots, or standing on a rock, I'd be dead," Cyrus finished her sentence. "But I'm not, and I wasn't, so all I have is a bad haircut and a graze wound. I was lucky."

"How did it happen?" Elizabeth asked. "Were you in a battle?"

Cyrus nodded. "We were over toward Suffolk, on the Nansemond River, at a place called Hill's Point. Our mission was to get the Rebels out of there and get the river open again for the Union ships. We outnumbered them by maybe five to four, but the fighting was still pretty fierce."

"Weren't you frightened?" Elizabeth asked, feeling foolish as soon as the question had slipped from her lips.

Cyrus grinned. "Scared witless, now that I think about it, but then, we didn't have much time to think. But to continue, we'd just about driven them out of there when I felt this burning heat on top of my head. I dropped back, and took off my cap. There was a hole clean through it, and this trail was blazed through my hair."

He paused to take a bite of his cornbread. "This is mighty tasty. You wouldn't believe the putrid mess the army calls food."

He returned to his story. "My buddy, Samuel Watters, helped me back to camp, to the doctor. He fixed me up as best he could and arranged for me to head home. I didn't want to come at first, because there was a lot of fighting going on in the area. But Sam rustled up some civilian clothes I could wear—I couldn't very well travel alone through Rebel territory wearing a Union uniform—and mostly I traveled at night, until I got closer to familiar terrain. Once I hit the mountains, I was home free." He shifted uneasily in his chair. "Well, almost home free."

"What is that supposed to mean?" Elizabeth's stomach lurched.

"Last evening, I was at this little saloon in a town about ten miles north. Don't even know the name of the place; it wasn't much more than the saloon, a few houses and half a dozen shuttered businesses. Anyway, I sat down to eat the first hot meal I'd had in days. Spent the last dime I had, too."

He pushed his chair back from the table. "That willow bark tea is already helping my headache. Or maybe it's just being off that damned horse. Sorry, Mamma," he added hastily. "Army language. I didn't mean to bring it home."

"I'm glad your head is feeling better," Catherine said. "Please go on."

"There were these two men sitting at a table behind me. At first, I didn't pay them no mind, but then I realized who they were. Or, more accurately, what they were."

"What were they?" Elizabeth asked.

"Bounty hunters. I'm sure of it, and one of them sounded really angry. Apparently he and his brother had been tracking one runaway for months. They'd nearly caught up to him, too, about a year ago, when they tangled with some guy on a horse. The guy's horse reared up and kicked the man's brother in the head, killing him."

Elizabeth blanched; she watched at Catherine's face turned as white as her own face felt.

"What else did you hear?" Catherine's voice was no more than a hoarse whisper.

"The horse killing his brother wasn't the all of it," Cyrus said. "Apparently, he'd taken a couple of shots at the fugitive, and wounded a bear in the process. The bear chased him and knocked him down. He beat her off with his rifle butt, but not before she took a good-sized bite out of his right thigh."

"Good for the bear," Elizabeth said dryly.

"My thoughts exactly," Cyrus agreed. "It's amazing the guy didn't bleed to death, or die of infection. But all she really did was make him mad. He told the other guy that he'd catch that no-good Malachi and the preacher man who helped him if it was the last thing he did."

Elizabeth clenched the table, forcing herself to take a deep breath. Her heart felt like it was going to rip right out of her chest and go running down the mountainside. "His name," she whispered. "Did you hear his name?"

"Hammer," Cyrus said. "Ephram Hammer." His eyes flicked from Elizabeth to Catherine, then back to Elizabeth once more. "But that doesn't surprise you, does it?"

She shook her head.

"The preacher man?"

"Your father," Catherine said. She continued talking, her voice becoming stronger as she told the story of the night William and Malachi met the Hammer brothers on the mountain; how William had sent Ephram and Bertram Hammer on a wild goose chase around the countryside to prevent their finding Malachi. How he'd not reined in his horse when it kicked at Bertram in the head, nor shot at the bear chasing Ephram from the woods. How Elizabeth had nursed Malachi back to health so he could once again slip through the night to help other fugitives find their way to freedom.

"You don't look surprised by all of this," Elizabeth said when her mother had finished talking.

"I'm not," Cyrus answered. "I knew when we built that room in the barn Papa intended to use it to hide runaway slaves, should the opportunity come his way." He looked closely at Elizabeth, and she could see the worry in his eyes. "This Malachi. He's become important to you."

"He's like family," Catherine answered.

For the second time that afternoon, Cyrus swore. "We have a problem," he said.

For the first time since she'd laid eyes on Malachi, Elizabeth wished with all her heart he was not due at the cabin that evening.

"I should have stayed back and killed that Hammer fellow when he left the saloon," Cyrus fumed. "I just wasn't sure, Mamma! The name Malachi didn't mean anything to me. He didn't call father by name, and I didn't know what had been going on here. No one wrote to me about it."

""We couldn't tell you, Cyrus, because if the letter had fallen into the wrong hands, we all would have been in trouble." Catherine frowned, then brightened. "I know what we'll do!" She jumped up from the table. "We'll take the lantern out of the window."

She rushed into the front room and yanked the beacon that signaled all was safe and well from its spot in the front window. "Malachi knows not to come if the lantern isn't in the window."

"He'll still come, Mamma," Elizabeth said, her voice heavy with fear. What if what Cyrus said was true? What if Ephram Hammer had returned to Hoffmann mountain to camp out and await Malachi's or Papa's return? What if he was lurking in the woods at the bottom of the mountain right now?

Chapter 13

August 15, 1863

It is with heavy heart I record the events of these past days. Having arrived home safely into the loving arms of my mother and sister, I learned the true story of the bounty hunters I encountered on my way home, that they were indeed searching for my father and the fugitive slave called Malachi. Furthermore, when Elizabeth and I stole a few private moments away from the watchful eyes and ears of our mother, I learned that my beloved sister had taken Malachi as her husband, and that she was now with child. She implored me to keep her secret until her husband arrived that evening, and then to help them break the news to our mother. I agreed to all that she asked.

Malachi arrived soon after the sun set in the west, bringing with him a man of tall stature and grim attitude. Elizabeth went with the two men to get the fugitive settled into the secret room in the barn. How to God I wish I had gone with them, that I had not been so weary I closed my eyes and dozed off inside the safety of the cabin! I awakened to the sound of shouting, then my sister screaming as rifle-fire exploded in the night...

I find it difficult to write of the grisly scene I encountered upon grabbing my service revolvers and running out the back door.....my beloved sister and her husband, dead in each others arms, with

Ephraim Hammer and his companion standing over their bodies. The fugitive Malachi had been attempting to help lay dead halfway across the yard, shot in the back.

Although a soldier in this tragic war that has ripped our great nation in two, I have never taken a human life. I aim to wound, not kill. But the scene before my eyes caused all sense of the sacredness of life to flee my mind, and with a roar, I let go a volley of gunfire that at once brought Ephraim Hammer into the company and judgment of his maker. His companion, a cowardly bastard, raced toward the shelter of the woods. He had no chance of escape, for a man who can aim to wound can also aim to kill, and I felled him before he had run twenty paces....

"Stop, James-Cyrus. I don't want to hear anymore." Cora's eyes were brimming over with tears. She pulled a handkerchief from the pocket of her trousers and blew her nose. "I always knew that story about her moving to Ohio had to be a bunch of hooey. I felt it in my bones, that something else had happened, something tragic. I just never knew what."

She got up from the porch chair and stretched. "I thought about going inside and fixing tea. I think I'll have a bourbon instead. To hell with the fact it's only eleven o'clock in the morning."

"I'll get it for you, Cora. You sit down." James-Cyrus ducked into the house, then returned with the bottle of bourbon and two glasses. "I'll join you."

They sipped their drinks in silence, watching the sheep graze in the meadow, Chance grazing peacefully among them. Somewhere in the distance, a wild turkey was raising a ruckus.

"Does it say where she's buried? She and Malachi? They're not in the family cemetery on your farm."

James-Cyrus nodded. "Cyrus buried them up in the clearing, next to the barn, so they could be together. The valley folk wouldn't have let Malachi be buried in a white cemetery if he'd brought them down the mountain."

"True," Cora nodded thoughtfully. She blew her nose again. "You know, James-Cyrus, part of me wonders why this has me so shook up. My daughter is dead, whether she died in Ohio or died on Hoffmann mountain. Either way, she's gone. But to have died so *violently*...that's what gets to me. And her being pregnant..."

"Did you know that part? That she was going to have a child?"

Cora shook her head. "That would have been one pretty baby, though."

He thought of his dream, how he had witnessed the events laid out by Cyrus in the journal. He couldn't tell Cora he'd seen what had transpired. But what if she was watching the cauldron when it happened? Her heart would break.

"Cora, you're not, I mean, you won't be able to..."

"Spit it out, James-Cyrus."

"It's just, I hope you aren't watching her in the cauldron when it happens."

"Watch my own child gunned down by a couple of thugs? No thank you." It was the first time in his entire life James-Cyrus heard bitterness in Cora's voice. "I intend to see her today, and say my good-byes. I can't risk accidentally watching something I don't think I could survive watching."

They slipped back into a comfortable silence. Cora's big black Merino ram was chasing Chance around the meadow, warning him away from the ewes. Cora laughed.

"That stupid ram has the sense of a black-eyed pea." She set down her glass.

"I can save them," James-Cyrus said quietly. "I can rescue them."

"Rescue who, the ewes? They don't need rescuing with old Ramesis watching over them," Cora said.

"I can rescue Elizabeth and Malachi. I can save them."

James-Cyrus raced Chance up the road at full speed. It had been a long time since he'd given the horse free reign, and Chance didn't let him down. They flew into the yard less than five minutes after jumping the fence surrounding Cora's sheep meadow.

After turning Chance out into the barnyard and hastily pitching some fresh hay and oats into her feed trough, James-Cyrus tore into the house, ideas forming in his head so quickly he had trouble sorting them out.

First, the fairy stone. He found it where he'd left it, on the coffee table in the living room. He pocketed it, then ran up the stairs two at a time to his bedroom.

The jar of fairy stones he had collected at Fairy Stone Park as a child still sat on his dresser. He opened the jar and dumped the whole lot onto his bed. Shifting through them, he selected the two that were as close in size and form to the magical one already in his pocket. Quickly counting, he realized there were only forty-three stones in all in he jar. He poured them all into a soft pouch, and ran back down the stairs to the kitchen.

Filling a water bottle and grabbing a couple of granola bars, he stuffed the pouch of stones, water, and snacks into his daypack. He was out the door and headed up the mountain less than thirty minutes after leaving Cora's porch, not stopping to explain his plan to her. Time was running out. For the first time in his life, he, like Cora, felt something in his bones, and knew his instincts were right.

He arrived at the cabin in record time, panting and sweating. He desperately wanted to cool off in the creek, but it was getting late in the day, and he didn't want to get caught on the mountain when night fell.

He spilled the fairy stones out of the pouch onto a flat rock near the front stairs. Then, pocketing one, he climbed the stairs and opened the door to the cabin.

Nothing but cobwebs and dust greeted him.

Returning to the rock, he placed the fairy stone back in the pouch and pocketed another. Forty-three times he climbed the stairs and opened the door. Forty-three times the cabin mocked him with its emptiness.

Frustrated, he sat on the rock. He wanted to go inside, to warn Elizabeth of the danger lurking in the woods. But she'd think him a raving lunatic. And what if Malachi was there? He'd tried to shoot him the last time. He didn't think Malachi could kill him, but he wasn't willing to take the chance.

He'd have to think of something else. It was getting late; the sun was already partially hidden behind the mountain. He had to leave, and leave now.

"I'll think of something, Elizabeth," he said to the cabin. "I'll be back. I promise."

He made it only halfway down the mountain before it got too dark for him to see. He knew better than to try to continue, for if he tripped over a rock or root and fell, or if he startled a rattlesnake on the hunt, he could be seriously injured or worse.

He leaned against a tree near the creek and pulled his solar blanket from his daypack. It wasn't very thick, nor did it provide any cushioning from the hard ground, but it would keep him warm and dry. He wished he'd packed more than just a couple granola bars in his pack. Oh well. He was hungry, but he certainly wouldn't starve to death overnight.. He squirmed around until he found a reasonably comfortable position and let the exhaustion of the day overtake him. He was asleep in five minutes.

He dreamed he was in the forest, watching as a young woman slept, her back to a tree just across the creek from him. She looked injured and feverish, and slept fitfully.

"Corrine, Corrine…" *He heard a voice coming from an old chestnut stump, dead and decaying for decades and aglow with foxfire, in the shape of an elderly crone.*

"Corrine, Corrine…"

"I'm here, Grandmother."

"Corrine…open your eyes!"

The woman opened her eyes and faced the foxfire, then bowed her head. *"Am I dead, then, too?"*

The foxfire crone chuckled. *"No, my child. You are not dead. But you have stumbled upon the ancient fairy magic, and your life has been forevermore changed."*

"William, my children…"

"What has become of them I cannot say," *the foxfire said.*

"Cannot, or will not? Do you not know?"

"Alas, it is not within my power to speak of things that have transpired," the foxfire replied. "I cannot tell you what has happened. This you must learn for yourself. But this I can say to you: Believe what you see."

"But I don't understand, Grandmother! Everything is wrong; everything is changed!" A tear slid down the woman's cheek.

"Everything has changed," the foxfire agreed. "And changed forevermore. But listen to my words, grandchild of my heart, and remember. The day will come when a grave wrong will be righted, if what was torn asunder is reunited."

"Remember what? Grandmother, you're speaking in riddles, and I don't understand!"

The foxfire began to flicker and fade. "What was torn asunder must be reunited; only then will this grave wrong be righted."

"Grandmother, don't leave me. I don't know what I'm supposed to do. Grandmother!"

"Remember, Corrine. What was torn asunder must be reunited..."

James-Cyrus awakened with a start. Dawn's first light was filtering through the trees; he could make out the earth and trees and rocks around him.

He had to get home, and to Cora. He had to tell her the dream, and see if it made any sense to her. He was sure the key to saving Elizabeth from her gruesome fate was hidden in the message of the dream.

He just needed to figure out how.

James-Cyrus didn't even bother to go inside his house to shower or change his clothes. Instead, he tossed his daypack up on the porch and, ignoring Chance's insistent nickering, jumped in his car and took off down the road for Cora's.

The fact that none of his fairy stones held magic, while disappointing, didn't really surprise him that much. They all felt cold to the touch, not warm like the magical stone.

But his dream, the dream of the foxfire crone. That meant something. Until now, his dreams had been of the cabin and what transpired there. How was this dream connected to the earlier ones? He had to find out, and he was sure Cora held the answers.

"I was expecting you," she said as he joined her on the porch. "I've made breakfast."

"Thanks, I'm starved," he said, collapsing into a chair. "I had only a couple of granola bars yesterday." He suddenly realized 'starved' didn't come close to what he was feeling.

"Well, don't get too comfortable. We can bring it out here, but you need to give me a helping hand."

Cora had fixed a feast: fresh banana nut bread, yogurt with fruit compote, a frittata with red peppers, asparagus, and sweet potatoes, and strong coffee laced with chicory. James-Cyrus gave her an appreciative hug. "You've outdone yourself. This looks marvelous."

"Well, I had to do something to occupy my time, waiting for you to come back." She picked up the tray with the coffee and flatware, and nodded at the larger tray of food. "You carry that one."

As they sat on the porch eating their breakfast, James-Cyrus told Cora how he had tried but failed to gain entry to the cabin with his fairy stone collection. "My hope was, if I could find more stones that worked, I'd have enough so I could bring Elizabeth and Malachi back into the future—into what is now—with me," he explained.

Cora nodded vaguely. "A noble thought. Why just them?"

"I thought about that," he said. "I can't bring your son to you, because if he comes into the now, I won't be here to have gone back in time to save Elizabeth. Sounds complicated, but it makes sense."

"You're right," she sighed. "I'd love to see my son again, but if he isn't there to meet his wife, Nathaniel won't be born—"

"Which means Granddaddy won't have been born, which means my father won't have been born, which means *I* won't be born. We'd be changing history."

"But since Elizabeth and Malachi died on the mountain, their baby was never born. If they made the time leap with you, it wouldn't affect descendants already born, because there weren't any."

"Right. But there's more to what happened yesterday." He quickly described the dream he'd had while sleeping in the forest. "The dream is connected to all of this, isn't it?" he asked. "After all, it was you in the dream. The foxfire crone called you 'Corrine.'"

Cora swallowed a bite of banana bread and nodded. "It happened just as you dreamed. The foxfire crone, as you call her, was my grandmother. She came to me the night I...the night it happened, when I was stumbling around lost in the woods."

"What do you think it means, 'What was torn asunder must be reunited; only then can this grave wrong be righted?'"

Cora paused. "Well, at first I thought it meant I'd be somehow reunited with William and Cyrus and Elizabeth. But then, when I found my cauldron in the shed and was able to watch Elizabeth in the water, I decided that's what it meant—that I had been reunited with my cauldron, and thus was able to at least watch my daughter grow up, righting the grave wrong of me being taken away from her."

"Sounds logical," James-Cyrus agreed. "But I don't see why the Grandmother came to me in my dream, then. My other dreams have been things you didn't already know, right?"

"Right."

They finished their breakfast, then walked out toward the meadow. James-Cyrus pulled the fairy stone from his pocket. "I wish the damned thing could be cloned. Maybe then the magic would spread to the clones."

He'd walked five paces ahead before he realized Cora had stopped. He backtracked to where she stood, frozen. "What? Cora, what are you thinking?"

"Oh, James-Cyrus, that's it! You're a genius; you just figured it out!" She threw her arms around him and squeezed him so tightly he nearly lost his breath.

"If you say, so," he said. "But, um, just so we're on the same page, do you mind telling me what I figured out?"

"Get in the car. You're taking me into the forest. Don't worry, not all the way to the top; even I know my limits."

"Fine, I'll take you. Do you mind if I ask why, just to reassure me you haven't gone and lost your mind?"

Cora hopped into the front passenger seat of the car as James-Cyrus started the engine. "We don't have to clone the fairy stone," she said, a triumphant smile on her face. "It already has two."

As they made their way up the path, Cora told James-Cyrus about the day she found the fairy stone. "It was in a cluster of three, and an odd cluster at that," she said. "You know how they normally are all stuck together in a jumbled cluster? Well, these three were arranged in a perfect triangle, each stuck to the base rock at the bottom of the cross. The whole thing struck me as magical and strange at the time, partly because I'd never seen or heard of a fairy stone. Seems even more magical now that I know how they actually form."

"I've never seen a cluster like that, either," James-Cyrus agreed.

"Now, if we can just find the rocky crevasse where I hid the other two." Her voice was tinged with both hope and desperation. It was about halfway between the creek and the trail, but the mountain has changed so much since then. The creek's course is different, and I don't know if this even is the same trail."

James-Cyrus stopped, and held out his hand for Cora to stop, too. "We can figure this out," he said. "I'm sure we can. What were you doing that day you found the stones?"

Cora thought a moment. "Harvesting slippery elm bark and picking morels. It was the first time I'd been out of the house since Elizabeth had been born."

"There's a grove of slippery elm over this way," James-Cyrus said, turning off the trail. "I know where it is because Granddaddy and I used to morel hunt there in the spring ourselves. There's a different trail leading to it; do you want to go back and start over, or bushwhack?"

"Bushwhack. We've wasted enough time." She cursed under her breath as a briar caught her; James-Cyrus pulled it out of her way. "I can't believe I'd forgotten about the other stones all these years."

They bushwhacked through the undergrowth for about ten minutes, ignoring the brambles, avoiding the poison ivy. Finally, they arrived at the stand of slippery elm.

"Does anything look familiar, Cora?"

"Quiet a moment." She closed her eyes, tilting her head, listening. "The creek is over this way," she said, taking off faster than she had been able to walk in years.

They arrived minutes later at the creek. Cora walked up and down the bank, studying the rocks. "I think it was here," she said, studying a large flat stone at water's edge. I think this is where I washed off the fairy stones, and where I dropped them." She whirled around. "Which means the rock where I hid the two I didn't take is over there somewhere." She pointed up stream and away from the bank.

For thirty minutes they searched up the stream bank and back down, looking in every crack and crevasse of every boulder for the fairy stones. They turned up nothing but an empty bird nest and, once, startled a common watersnake out of its hiding place.

Discouraged, James-Cyrus slumped to the ground and leaned his head back against a rock. "It's no use. The land has changed so much. We could be miles from where you hid those fairy stones. Or, they might have washed away when the stream flooded." He wiped a trickle of sweat off his forehead. "I'm sorry, Cora. We tried. I really thought we'd find them."

But Cora wasn't listening. Instead, she was staring in a crack in the rock, just above where James-Cyrus sat.

"We did find them," she whispered.

Gently she pulled the fairy stones from the shelter where they had been resting for more than one hundred forty years. "Feel them," Cora said as she placed them in his hands.

"They're warm, like the other one," James-Cyrus replied. "Is that a good sign?"

"'What was torn asunder must be reunited; only then can this grave wrong be righted,'" Cora whispered. "All these years I thought 'torn asunder' meant me and my family. But it's the fairy stones that were torn asunder—that's what the Grandmother meant!"

"And now that they have been reunited, you have the power to reunite with your daughter?"

Cora smiled so broadly her eyes nearly disappeared into her weathered, wrinkled face, then turned and walked toward the slippery elm grove. She called back to him over her shoulder, "Well, are you coming?"

He caught up with her in four long strides. "How am I going to convince them to come with me?" he asked as they turned down the trail that led from the slippery elm grove to the farm below. "Malachi nearly shot me last time. This time he might really shoot me, if he finds me telling his wife I'm a relative from the future whose come to save her life. It sounds preposterous, even to me, and I'm the one doing it."

"We'll need my sister's help," Cora replied.

"Catherine? But Cora, how are we going to get her to help? At least Elizabeth and Malachi have seen my strange comings and goings. Catherine hasn't, and I doubt seriously Elizabeth has said anything to her."

"You're right on all counts." Cora stopped a moment to catch her breath. "But Catherine has some understanding of mountain magic. She's an herb woman, like I was, or am, rather. The Grandmother taught her about spirits just the same as she taught me. If anything, Catherine was a more adept student of hers than I was, because she was a few years older."

"Understood. But my question remains, how are we going to get her help?"

"I have an idea," Cora said, heading down the trail once again. "But we're going to have to work quickly. We don't have that many hours left until it gets dark."

Seven o'clock found Cora and James-Cyrus back on Hoffmann mountain, at the brook where both had met the Grandmother. In the dwindling light James-Cyrus unpacked the backpacking gear they'd brought along—a two-person tent, sleeping bags, and some food—while Cora gathered wood to build a campfire. Then, they waited.

They did not talk. For Cora, it had been a long, exhausting day wrought with emotion. If they were right, if the twin fairy stones held the same magic as the one she'd broken off so many years before, she could be reunited with her daughter by this time tomorrow. She refused to let her mind wander to the dark corner of her mind where Elizabeth and Malachi lay murdered in the backyard of what once had been her home.

James-Cyrus had carefully cut the twin stones apart from their base. "They're still warm," she had said when he placed them in her hands. "That's good." The three fairy stones now were tucked securely into the zipped pocket of James-Cyrus's jacket.

She looked at James-Cyrus lovingly. She'd helped Samuel raise the boy, and she loved him like a son. That wouldn't change when Elizabeth came. A mother's ability to love always expanded when a new child arrived. She knew it didn't matter if that child was a baby or a young adult.

And a grandchild! She imagined a sticky-fingered, chubby-thighed tot toddling toward her, diapers sagging, wanting to be picked up and held. Was it a boy? Girl? It didn't matter. All that mattered was that the baby be given a chance for life, a chance they wouldn't get if James-Cyrus wasn't successful.

The fire was growing dim. She turned to James-Cyrus. "It's time," she said.

She stirred the coals in the fire while James-Cyrus laid out the items she'd packed from her kitchen. "Are you ready?" she asked.

He nodded. "I don't know what to do. I've never done anything like this before."

"That's all right," she assured him. "Just follow my lead. Be reverent and respectful, and don't talk unless spoken to. Do you understand?"

He nodded his assent, and the ritual began.

"Grandmother of old, we come to you with these offerings of tobacco and cornmeal. With these gifts we honor your memory." Cora threw some tobacco on the fire and poured the cornmeal on the earth beside it. The flames flared.

"Grandmother, I have with me James-Cyrus, also of our ancient lineage, and whom you visited in his dreams here in this very spot where we now honor you. I ask that you come to us again and speak, that we might gain insight through your wisdom."

The forest was dark; not even the stars were out. James-Cyrus could see no farther than a few feet beyond the glowing embers of the fire. The chestnut stump loomed at the very edge of the darkness like some sort of macabre specter. He squirmed uncomfortably. What had he let Cora talk him into?

Cora threw another pinch of tobacco on the hot coals. "Grandmother, we have found the two fairy stones once paired with the one I took so long ago. What was torn asunder has been reunited. I ask your help now on righting the grave wrong committed those many years ago."

"Corrine." James-Cyrus nearly fell over backward as the inchoate whisper floated from the chestnut stump. *"Beloved granddaughter, now known as Cora, and James-Cyrus, the chosen one."* The tree sprang to life as the bright yellow-green glow of foxfire lit the night.

"Grandmother." Cora bowed her head. James-Cyrus followed suit. He didn't know if he should be grateful for the Grandmother's appearance or scared out of his wits.

"Grandmother," Cora continued, "My daughter, your great-granddaughter, is in mortal peril. Unless we can find a way to rescue her, she and her husband and unborn child will die."

"And what is it you summoned me here for, child?" the Grandmother asked gently.

"We have the magic fairy stones, all three of them. They have been brought together once again, as you instructed," Cora said. "We need your help so that Elizabeth and Malachi will come back with James-Cyrus when he goes for them."

"And what makes you think I can help you?" The foxfire Grandmother flared so brightly James-Cyrus had to shield his eyes.

"Because you told me that night I journeyed to this time and place from my own that when what was torn asunder was reunited, this grave wrong could be righted."

She turned to James-Cyrus. "Give me the stones," she whispered.

He unzipped his pocket and handed her the three fairy stones. She held her hand out toward the Grandmother. "See? All three of them."

"The grave wrong I spoke of was your taking the sacred stones to begin with," the Grandmother said sharply. "They must be returned to where they were found. Then all will be well once again in the fairy world."

Cora's shoulders sagged. "All will be well in the *fairy* world? What of my world, Grandmother? What of my daughter and her unborn child?"

The Grandmother's flare settled down. "The fairy stones marked the final resting place of a beloved fairy queen. When you took the stones that marked her grave, the fairies were most displeased. When all is not well in the fairy world, all is not well in your world either, nor in the world your daughter now inhabits. Look around you! What do you see? Rotting corpses where mighty chestnuts once stood, destroyed by a killing blight. Look at the brown spots on the leaves of those trees still here, burned by the very rains themselves. And where is brother wolf? Have you seen him lately?"

Tears welled up in Cora's eyes, yet they did not spill. "I am truly sorry if I offended the fairy world, Grandmother," she said. "I did not know what I was doing."

She got up off the ground where she was seated, and slowly walked over to the Grandmother. She knelt before her, bowing her head once again. "But you *will* help me get my daughter to safety. Do you know why?"

She didn't wait for the Grandmother to answer. "You will help me because as much as you loved this mountain in life, as much reverence and respect you had for the fairy world, you loved me more." She looked up at the blazing tree. "*You loved me more.*"

The foxfire died down to a faint, warm glow. Cora knelt steadfast.

"Very well, Granddaughter," the Grandmother said. "Do not despair, for you are right. I did love you more than the mountains. I still do, for a grandmother's love cannot be extinguished by death like a flame is by water." She flared again, ever so slightly. "Have you an idea as to how we shall accomplish this daring mission?"

"I do, Grandmother," Cora said. "You could go to Elizabeth in her dreams, and Catherine in hers, as you did to James-Cyrus. Tell them both Elizabeth and Malachi must accompany James-Cyrus, or they will perish."

The Grandmother flared brightly. "I believe that might work. Yes, I will go to Elizabeth and Catherine. James-Cyrus, come here!"

Trembling, James-Cyrus joined Cora in front of the Grandmother tree and knelt.

"This is a dangerous undertaking for you, young man, for if they do not listen to me—and I cannot force them to listen and believe—you will be in grave danger, for if you lose the fairy stone, you will be forever stuck in the past. Worse yet, if you are killed—"

"I mean no disrespect, Grandmother, but wouldn't I simply be born once again when the time came?" he asked.

The Grandmother guffawed. "Those among the living have such quaint ideas of what happens between the worlds of the past, present, and future," she laughed. "It really is quite endearing."

Trying not to be annoyed, James-Cyrus stood up and looked the Grandmother in the eye. "Nevertheless, I will do whatever is in my power to help Elizabeth," he said. "I'll bring her back to Cora or die trying."

"And why would you put your life on the line for Elizabeth, who is but a stranger to you?"

James-Cyrus looked down at Cora, still on her knees. He took her by the hands and pulled her to her feet before answering. "Because, Grandmother, I love Cora more than the mountains, too."

The foxfire dimmed to a low simmer once again. "Very well said, young man, very well said." The Grandmother made a noise that sounded like she was clearing her throat. "Go, then, tomorrow. I will pay both Elizabeth and Catherine a visit this very night. And may all the spirits of the forest be with you, James-Cyrus, as you undertake this dangerous quest."

"Thank you, Grandmother," Cora said. "I am grateful."

The foxfire dimmed once more; the Grandmother was leaving. They had already turned back toward their tent when a thought popped into James-Cyrus's mind.

"Grandmother, don't go yet!" he turned back to the chestnut stump. The foxfire flickered dimly.

"Yes, James-Cyrus?" Her voice sounded distant, and had an echo-like quality about it.

"When you first came tonight, you called me 'the chosen one.' What did you mean by that?"

The foxfire beamed brightly, and the Grandmother's laughter once again filled the air. "James-Cyrus, dear, boy, who do you think gave you all those dreams throughout your life that led you to the cabin and Elizabeth to begin with?"

Chapter 14

William and Malachi arrived at the cabin under cover of darkness. The men looked tense, and after Elizabeth dished them up bowls of stew and dumplings, they sat at the table to talk.

"You all know Jeremiah, my cousin. He's in trouble," Malachi said.

"Your cousin? What happened?" Catherine asked.

"He was spotted a couple of nights ago by Ephraim Hammer and his new partner—I don't know his name," William said. "I found out when a contact of mine overhead them in a tavern just north of here."

"Why, that must be the same place I saw them," Cyrus said. "Why didn't Hammer take out Jeremiah then and there?"

Malachi grimaced. "Because of me," he said. "Hammer knew if he followed Jeremiah, he'd lead him to me. And as far as he's concerned, I'm a bigger fish to catch, so to speak."

"But I thought the bounty on your head was only fifty dollars!" Elizabeth cried.

"It is. But at this point, it isn't the money as far as Hammer is concerned. It's revenge for his brother's death. He wants my hide."

William reached across the table and took his wife's hand. "And probably, mine, too," he said.

"No, William…" Catherine's voice was a whisper.

"I feel responsible for this mess," Malachi said. "If it weren't for me, none of you would be in any danger right now."

"Nonsense, Malachi." Catherine found her voice. "There's a war going on, and even though there hasn't been any action within twenty miles of here, everyone in Virginia is in danger."

"No one is to blame," William said firmly. "What we have done, what we *all* have done, was the right thing. " He turned to Malachi. "What we need to do now, though, is find Jeremiah and get him across the mountain to safety. Do you know where to find him?"

Malachi nodded. "We're to meet up two night's hence, at our usual place. We can stop here until it's safe to travel, or until Hammer and his crony catch up with us. I can use a gun as well as any man, and Jeremiah can too. That'd make four of us—you, Cyrus, me, and Jeremiah—to two of them. I don't think they'd fight us under those odds, do you?"

"Five," Elizabeth said. "I can use a gun, too."

"We don't have that many weapons, sweetheart," William said. "I know you can shoot, and shoot well, too, but—"

"But I'm a woman," she said flatly, crossing her arms and resting them on her belly.

Her belly. She could feel its new, slight roundedness, a roundness created to protect the child, Malachi's child, that lay nestled inside her. She couldn't put their child at risk. But Malachi's life was in danger; what would she do if he were captured or killed? What would become of her baby? Worry engulfed her like a blizzard in February, sending chills down her spine and a wave of nausea through her gut.

"I'm going to be sick," she moaned as she jumped up from the table and staggered out the back door. She made it only a few steps before the bile rose in her throat. She sank to her knees and vomited as the world went black around her.

She awakened the next morning, in her bed in the loft. Catherine and Malachi were by her side, and Catherine was taking a compress from her forehead and replacing it with a fresh, cold one.

"Welcome back, my love," her mother said gently. "I was getting worried about you."

Elizabeth tried to sit up, then sank back into the pillows with a groan. "My head aches. What happened to me?"

Catherine squeezed her hand. "You vomited, then fainted. Don't worry, it isn't an uncommon set of circumstances in pregnant women."

Elizabeth's heart jumped, then sank. Her mother knew. Malachi knew, and she hadn't been the one to tell him. "Cyrus," she said.

Malachi leaned over and kissed her cheek. "Cyrus. He said the two of you had a talk before your father and I arrived yesterday, and that you were going to tell me about the child last evening. He said you told him first so he could give you some moral support when you told Catherine and William."

"Not that you needed any," Catherine said crisply. "Your father and I aren't blind. We could see you two were in love."

"But you never said anything."

"What was there to say? You know the color of a man's skin is of no importance to us. The two of you couldn't legally be married, although perhaps when this war ends that will change. In the meantime, we thought it best to simply keep quiet and allow you two young people to do what you thought best. You've always had a good head on your shoulders, Elizabeth. We trust your judgment." Catherine turned her gaze toward her son-in-law. "And yours too, Malachi."

Elizabeth found her husband's hand and held it tightly. "So you told them of our wedding vows?"

Malachi nodded. "Every little detail, down to the raven cawing in the tree."

"It sounds like it was beautiful," Catherine said. "Grandmother would have approved. Your father, though, would like to bestow his formal blessing on your marriage in front of us all, though, if you will allow him to."

"We'd be honored," Malachi said.

That evening, standing beneath the hemlock tree at the edge of the clearing and attended by every star in the universe, Elizabeth and Malachi repeated their wedding vows before William, Catherine, and Cyrus.

"What love has joined together, let no man nor war put asunder," William said when they were finished. "Malachi, you may kiss your bride. Usually I add, 'for the first time,' but considering what's growing in my daughter's belly, I reckon I'm too late for that," he added dryly.

Elizabeth ignored her father's gentle teasing. She turned her face up to her husband's, and met his lips with her own, no hiding, no secrecy. Her family knew. They knew, they understood, they *approved.*

The call of a catbird from the forest darkness interrupted her reverie. Malachi, too, looked uneasy. "We better all get back inside," he said.

Elizabeth dreamed she was in the forest with Catherine. It was dark, and they were beside the creek, kneeling before a chestnut tree stump ablaze with foxfire.

"Elizabeth, Catherine, listen and listen well."

"We're listening, Grandmother," Catherine said.

"Dear granddaughter, and dearest great-granddaughter, I come to you because Elizabeth and Malachi are in grave danger," the Grandmother said. "Unless they flee tomorrow night, by next day's dawn both will lie dead in each others arms."

"But Grandmother!" Catherine cried. "How can my daughter flee? She is with child. She needs me."

The Grandmother chuckled kindly. "A girl does need her mother when she herself becomes one," she agreed. "But rest assured, if Elizabeth and Malachi go with the stranger called James-Cyrus when he comes for them, Elizabeth will indeed deliver a healthy child into the hands of her mother—the mother into whose hands you yourself delivered Elizabeth."

"Corrine?" Catherine gasped. *"But Grandmother, my sister has been dead these twenty years, gone without a trace."*

"Corrine is not dead, but in another realm," the Grandmother said, *"the realm of the future, from where James-Cyrus comes. Believe what you see. Send Elizabeth and Malachi with James-Cyrus, who is your kin. Only then will they be safe."*

"Grandmother, she is my only daughter!"

"I know, child," the Grandmother soothed. *"But 'tis better to have your only daughter alive in another place than dead in thy home, in the arms of her beloved."*

"I'm afraid, Grandmother," Elizabeth said. *"I don't know what will become of us."*

"Dear Elizabeth, great-granddaughter, it is not within the power of any human to know what will become of them," she said. *"But this much is certain: If you do not go with James-Cyrus, you will die, and the child you carry will not be born."*

The foxfire began to fade. *"Remember, Elizabeth and Malachi must go or they will die. Believe what you see. Believe what you see."*

Malachi left at daybreak the next morning. "Why do you have to go so soon?" Elizabeth pleaded. "You said Jeremiah is meeting you tonight. Please. Stay with me. I had such a frightening dream last night; I can't bear for you to leave me alone."

Malachi held his young wife's head between his hands, his fingers entwined in her dark curls. "I can't risk not being there when Jeremiah arrives," he said gently. "He's in trouble, and he may already be hiding there, waiting for me to come. I've got to get to him before Hammer does.

You're not alone. Your mother and father, and your brother, all are here with you."

"But what if it's Hammer you find there, and not Jeremiah?" she sobbed. "He'll kill you."

"I'm not going to let Hammer kill me, sweetheart." He kissed away a tear that ran down her face, then placed a hand on her stomach. "I've got too much waiting for me back here to let him do that."

He turned to William, Catherine, and Cyrus, who stood silently in the doorway, waiting to say their own good-byes. "You take care of my wife for me until I get back."

"Of course," Cyrus said. "Be safe, Malachi."

"I'll be back this evening with Jeremiah." He kissed Elizabeth gently on the lips. "I promise. I'll be back."

Chapter 15

James-Cyrus bounded up the trail like a deer. He tried to be vigilant about his surroundings, as Cora warned, but the farther up the trail he went, the more difficult it became, for the forest began to change.

Chestnut stumps gave way to giant chestnut trees, a sea of behemoths beneath which tulip trees and hemlocks struggled for light and life. Even the stream looked different, running a slightly different course than he remembered.

He forged onward, even when the trail dwindled to nothing more than a deer track, following his inner compass, his instincts, to find the cabin and Elizabeth.

He patted the zipped pocket of his jacket, reassuring himself the fairy stones were securely inside. Not that he doubted it, considering the changes he was witnessing in the forest.

He hoped the Grandmother had gotten through to Elizabeth and Catherine in their dreams. *A grandmother's love cannot be extinguished by death like a flame is by water,* she'd said.

But a mother's love was surely as strong or stronger than that of a grandmother. Would Catherine let her daughter go just because the Grandmother said to?

He stopped to catch his breath, and removed a packet of papers from another pocket. Here were photocopies of Cyrus's diary, a photo of Cora, and a photo of the bowl and pitcher set that had once been Corrine's. That had been Cora's idea. "If she sees the bowl and pitcher and the journal, how can she doubt you have them?" she said. "And I still look like the Corrine she'd remember. I'm just gray and wrinkled. She'll know it's me." She didn't sound quite as certain about that. As for James-Cyrus, he wasn't certain the papers would make the leap unchanged, but nothing ventured, nothing gained, he supposed.

The sound of voices off to his right shook him out of his contemplations. Silently, he slipped behind a chestnut tree and listened. Two men, heading his way.

"They's up here somewhere, Crawley," one man said. "A pint of whiskey says we find 'em by nightfall."

"Sure, Hammer, whatever you say," the other man said. "But keep yer whiskey. I just want my share of the reward."

"Damn the reward," Hammer growled. "I just want to see that coward Malachi and preacher man on their knees, beggin' for their lives. And if I get me a piece of a bear in the process, all the better."

"How'd you know if it's the same bear what bit you? Don't seem to make no sense to me."

"Don't make no difference to me—one dead bear's as good as another," Hammer said.

Focus, James-Cyrus, focus! His thoughts were running a mile a minute and in all different directions. He had to calm down; had to form a plan. Hammer and his partner were too close. Too close not only to him, but to the cabin and his family there.

The men were now in plain sight. The one in the lead he assumed was Hammer. He couldn't have been more than five-six in height, James-Cyrus guessed; the one Hammer called Crawley was somewhat shorter. Both were scrawny, and their clothes sagged on them. They carried their rifles carelessly at their sides, not aimed forward like they were ready to shoot.

He could take them. He was sure of it.

"You got a plan, once we find this cabin?" Crawley asked.

"Sure I got a plan," Hammer said with a chuckle. "We'll set fire to his barn. That'll draw 'em out of the house. Then they're ours."

"Good plan." Crawley leaned against a tulip tree. "Gotta stop here, Hammer, my feets about to kill me."

"I told you not to steal them boots, you fool," Hammer said. "Yer other ones was bigger."

"But these ain't got no holes in 'em," Crawley said. "The other 'uns was full of holes."

"Well, these are gonna have holes now," Hammer growled. "Give 'em to me."

Tossing their rifles aside, the two men plopped down on a rock, and Crawley removed his boots. Hammer pulled a knife from a sheath on his hip and began hacking at the leather toes.

"Hey, those is good boots!" Crawley protested. "Whatcha gotta go and ruin—"

"Drop the knife, Hammer. And both of you, hands in the air."

Hammer slowly turned to face James-Cyrus, knife still in hand. He dropped it when James-Cyrus stuck his own rifle barrel in his face.

"Crawley, you fool, why weren't you watchin—"

"Me? I thought you was—"

"Shut up, both of you." James-Cyrus took a step back, covering both men with the gun. He'd counted on the guns being loaded; from the reaction of the two bounty hunters, lady luck had been with him.

"You, Hammer. Against that tree, on the ground. Move!" James-Cyrus shouted when Hammer didn't jump.

Hammer did as he was told, moving to the sapling James-Cyrus pointed to and sinking to the ground.

"Now you, Crawley. Tie him up with this." James-Cyrus tossed him the nylon cording from the hood of his jacket. "Hands behind him, around that little tree, nice and tight."

He watched as Crawley tied Hammer's hands together. "Now, his feet." He handed Crawley the shoelace from his right hiking boot. "Good."

He pulled the shoelace from his remaining boot. "Now you, over here." He pointed to a sapling ten feet from the one Hammer was tied to. "Hands behind you."

This would be the tricky part, James-Cyrus realized, because he'd have to set down the gun to tie Crawley up. He thought for a moment. "Drop your pants."

"What?" Crawley balked. "You ain't..."

"I said, drop your pants!" James-Cyrus roared. "Off with them, now."

Sweating, Crawley did as he was told.

"Now, on the ground, and tie your legs together with your pants. In a knot, there, that's good. Okay, hands behind the tree."

When Crawley had awkwardly complied, James-Cyrus set the gun down. Quickly, he wrapped his shoelace around the shaking man's wrists and the tree.

"There. That ought to hold you both for a while." He wished he had brought stronger rope, but he did the best with what he had. Still, it wouldn't hold the men for long, of that he was sure. He had to move, and quickly.

"You guys so much as twitch for the next two hours and you're dead. I'll be watching. Do you understand?"

Not waiting for their answer, he turned and bounded up the mountainside.

When he'd run about five hundred feet, he stopped, panting. He'd run straight up hill, away from Hammer and Crawley, as fast as he could. He had to get to the cabin. But first he had to catch his breath.

He was near the cabin, he could sense it. He'd have been there by now if he hadn't stumbled across the bounty hunters, although, considering how close they had been, it was a blessing. He'd slowed them down a bit. He couldn't kill them. He'd never killed another human being; in fact, he'd never held a gun before. He couldn't have pulled the trigger.

The guns. "Shit!" He swore at the top of his lungs. "What an idiot you are, JC!"

He'd left them by the men. He'd meant to bring both the rifles and the knife with him, but he'd been so frightened. He'd been operating on a mixture of fear and adrenaline, and not thinking clearly. All he could think about was disabling Hammer and Crawley and then getting as far away from them as possible.

Now he really had to move. The knife wasn't within their reach, but those laces wouldn't hold the men for long, and they'd be after not only Malachi and William, but him, too.

Ignoring his racing heart and shortness of breath, he plunged through the woods.

He didn't run far before the hemlock tree that marked the edge of the cabin came into view. He burst out of the woods and into the clearing, racing as fast as his legs would carry him up the stairs and through the door.

Elizabeth and Catherine were sitting at the table. A man James-Cyrus recognized as his great-great-grandfather Cyrus slept in a chair, his head wrapped in a blood-tinged bandage.

Elizabeth got up from the table and hurried over to him. "James-Cyrus, you're back," she said. "Sit down, rest. Catch your breath."

He shook his head, still gasping for breath. "Can't. There's no time." He bent down, placing his hands on his knees, willing his racing heart to slow. Only then did he realize he was still in his hiking clothes, that he had not reverted to the uniform of a soldier. "On second, thought, I better sit for just a minute. But only a minute." He sank into the chair next to Catherine, who was as pale as the full moon.

"James-Cyrus, this is my mother—"

"Catherine," he finished her sentence. "I know. Pleased to meet you, although I wish the circumstances were different." He held out his hand, but she didn't take it. She only stared, as if looking at a ghost.

"Believe what you see," she whispered.

He nodded. "The Grandmother."

Her eyes filled with tears. "Yes."

Elizabeth turned to her mother, wide-eyed. "I had a dream last night about the Grandmother," she said. "She said Malachi and I had to go with James-Cyrus or we'd die. She said, 'Believe what you see.'"

Catherine only whispered again, "Believe what you see."

"You were in my dream," Elizabeth cried. "Did you have the same dream?"

Catherine nodded.

James-Cyrus pulled the papers from his pocket. "I hope this will explain somewhat, Elizabeth. We don't have much time...Hammer and Crawley will be free and they're too close..."

"Hammer? How do you know Hammer?" Elizabeth asked sharply. Her eyes grew wide. "Malachi was right! You're one of them! You've given us away!"

"No, no! I'd never do that...Elizabeth, you just have to listen and trust me!" He spread the papers on the table.

The photocopy of Cyrus's journal was blank, but the photograph of Cora and the bowl and pitcher set remained intact.

"This bowl and pitcher set," James-Cyrus pointed to the identical set on a table in the corner, "is sitting in my bedroom of my house. It was painted by Esther Mae Hoffmann, your father's sister, as a wedding present when he married your mother. Your birth mother, Corrine."

Elizabeth paled. "How do you know that?"

James-Cyrus ignored the question. "And this," he said, pointing to the picture of Cora, "is your mother, Corrine. Cora, we call her."

"I've seen her before," Elizabeth whispered. "I've seen her in the water, in the cauldron."

"She's seen you too," he said. "I don't have time to explain. Is Malachi here? Where's Malachi?"

"He's in the barn." Catherine had found her voice. "And so is William. They're in the barn with Jeremiah."

"Do they have guns with them?"

Catherine shook her head.

"We need to get them inside, now," James-Cyrus said. "They said they were going to burn down the barn, to flush the men out of the house. We don't have much time!"

He jumped up from the table and grabbed for the rifle, but Elizabeth was a step ahead of him. "You told me you're a cattle farmer, remember?" she said. "Have you ever even fired a rifle? No? I didn't think so."

With that she claimed the rifle and hurried out the back door.

James-Cyrus turned back to Catherine. She was shaking Cyrus by the shoulder.

"Cyrus, Cyrus, wake up! There's trouble brewing." She turned to James-Cyrus. "You've come for my daughter and Malachi. Just like the Grandmother said in my dream."

James-Cyrus nodded.

"And if I don't let her go? Is what the Grandmother said in the dream true? What will happen to her if I don't let her go with you?"

"She and Malachi will be gunned down in your backyard by Hammer and Crowley. I've tied them up in the woods, but it won't stop them for long. We have to go *now*."

"And your certain."

"Yes. Cyrus wrote about it in his journal, which I have in my attic." He picked up the blank pages from the table. "I tried to bring a copy of it to show you, but the writing disappeared. I guess because it doesn't exist yet, if that makes any sense."

"None of this makes any sense." Catherine let out a sob. "But the Grandmother said to believe."

"I'm sorry. But it's the only way to save her life."

"And the rest of us?"

"Will live long, happy lives," James-Cyrus said firmly. He nodded his head toward the rousing Cyrus. "He's my great-great grandfather."

Elizabeth dashed across the yard toward the barn. She didn't know who James-Cyrus was, but she could see the desperation in his face.

And her mother. Catherine. They'd shared the same dream last night. That scared her more than James-Cyrus did.

She burst through the barn door and nearly plowed into the men. "We've got to get inside, now!" she cried. "Hammer and Crowley are coming!"

"Hide in the room, Jeremiah, Malachi," William ordered.

"No! They said they're going to burn down the barn," Elizabeth said. "Hurry, we have to run!"

They were halfway across the yard when Hammer and Crowley stepped out from behind the hemlock. "Hold it right there, Malachi, preacher man," Hammer yelled. "On yer knees!"

"Don't stop, Malachi," Elizabeth ordered. "Run for the house!" Malachi held his ground, but Jeremiah turned and fled. Elizabeth took aim and fired the rifle at the men. Crowley flinched, and blood streamed from his shoulder. "The bitch done shot me!" he yelled. He fired back.

"Jeremiah, no!" Malachi screamed, as his cousin crumpled to the ground. He pushed Elizabeth behind him. "Don't hurt her!" he shouted. "It's me you want. Don't shoot!"

Slowly, Hammer raised his gun. "On yer knees and say yer prayers, boy."

The three ran for the house. Elizabeth braced for the sound of gunshot as she ran, but heard instead a blood-curdling scream. As they reached the safety of the cabin, they turned to see a she-bear charging out of the wood, running full speed at Hammer and Crawley. Hammer took aim and fired, but the shot was wide. The men ran toward the hemlock tree, scampering up to the highest branches.

"Close the door, quickly!" William urged. Malachi bolted the door, then peered out its small window. "Those fools went up a tree. The bear's still after them."

Elizabeth hugged James-Cyrus. "You saved our lives," she said. "Thank you."

"I haven't saved anyone's life yet," James-Cyrus said, grimly. "You and Malachi must come with me."

"Come with you? But where?"

"Elizabeth, if you don't come—"

"Let me, James-Cyrus," Catherine said quietly. She turned to her daughter.

"The world is a magical place, Elizabeth. You know that. There are some things we can explain, and others we can't. What happened to your mother all those years ago is one of the things we couldn't explain. But here is James-Cyrus, telling us she is alive and well, waiting for you. And if you don't go with him, you and Malachi are going to die, here, tonight, at the hands of those two men."

"But we can take the men," Malachi protested, "There are more of us than there are of them."

"History says you died this night, and Elizabeth, too," James-Cyrus said. "That can change only if you come with me."

Shouts came from the yard; Cyrus peered out the window. "They've beaten off the bear. She's gone. They're coming!" he said.

William hugged his daughter. "Go," he said, his voice choked with emotion. "I don't understand this mountain magic, but I've seen enough of it to know it is real. Go. Be safe."

"I don't want to write your death in my journal, like James-Cyrus here says I wrote," Cyrus said, hugging his sister. "I'd rather you be alive somewhere else than dead here."

The men were pounding on the door. "Open up! We've got you cornered! We don't aim to hurt the women; it's the preacher man and Malachi we want." The door shook on its hinges. "Open up!"

"Say hello to my sister, for me," Catherine said, gazing at Elizabeth through tear-stained eyes. "Be well."

Elizabeth took Malachi's hand. "Do you trust me? Are you with me?"

Malachi looked at James-Cyrus. "In your world. Will Elizabeth and I be free? Can we live as husband and wife?"

James-Cyrus nodded. "Absolutely. Free, and legally wed as husband and wife."

"All right, then, what do we do?"

James-Cyrus pulled two of the fairy stones from his pocket and slipped one into the pocket of Elizabeth's dress, the other into Malachi's shirt. "Let's do it, then."

The back door was crumbling; the men outside had found the axe next to the wood pile. William and Cyrus both opened fire.

"Go!" Catherine cried, as she opened the front door and pushed James-Cyrus, Elizabeth, and Malachi out in a blaze of light.

Chapter 16

Cora paced back and forth across her front porch, every once in a while stopping to stare down the road, willing James-Cyrus, Elizabeth, and Malachi to appear. It was too soon, she told herself. It was too soon. Time was different when he went back.

Cyrus's journal was on the table, and she picked it up. The horrors of her daughter's death leapt from the pages; hastily she set it down. She clambered down the stairs toward the cauldron in the yard, thought the better of it, and slowly climbed back up the stairs to the porch.

She picked up her tea cup, but her hands were shaking so badly she could barely find her mouth. The tea was cold, anyway. She went into the house to fix a fresh cup. Chamomile this time. Her nerves couldn't take much more.

Tea brewed, she returned to the porch, carrying her knitting with her. She was making a baby blanket, pink and blue stripes, for her grandchild. A blanket, and booties, and little sweaters. She smiled. She was going to be busy.

Elizabeth and Malachi would live with her, of course. The house wasn't as large as the big one James-Cyrus lived in, but it had three bedrooms. Plenty of room for the family. Then, once they got used to their new world, their new surroundings, if they wanted, they could build a house of their own.

She reached for her tea, but her hand never made it to the cup. It froze over the journal. The letters were vanishing, and new writing was appearing in their stead. Cora held her breath, not daring to move until the writing had transformed completely.

The events of this past weeks have been so fantastic I almost dare not write them down, for fear I will be branded a lunatic, yet what I write I swear on my life is a true accounting.

Two men invaded the tranquility of our home and property, intent on the murder of my father and our family friend, Malachi, who recently took my beloved sister Elizabeth to wed. Elizabeth fought well, wounding one of the murderous vandals. But the pair was determined to spill the blood of my family, and God only knows if they would have succeeded had not an angel interceded, appearing in our home and sweeping Elizabeth and Malachi away in a blaze of white light at the very moment the would-be killers burst through our back door. Father and I were ready, and those who would have done us harm instead met their own fates, and now lie buried shallow graves beyond the clearing.

I cannot but hope Elizabeth and Malachi have found peace and happiness wherever they may be. As for us, we have received news that General Lee has surrendered. This tragic war has drawn to a close. Father and I have agreed the best thing to do is to burn this cabin to the ground and move to the valley below. Nothing remains for us here.

Cora set the journal down. So William and Cyrus had burned the cabin, or so it would appear. But if that were true, how did Samuel and James-Cyrus after him find it up on the mountain? It didn't make sense.

'Believe what you see. Believe what you see.' The Grandmother's words echoed in Cora's head. She understood. It did make sense.

"Thank you, Grandmother," she whispered.

She got up from the porch and walked down to the cauldron, no longer afraid. She watched as the black ring expanded, erasing her window to the past. But there was no sorrow in her heart as the image before her disappeared, for what she saw was James-Cyrus, Elizabeth, and Malachi walking down the trail toward the valley and home.

Chapter 17

Cora, James-Cyrus, Elizabeth, and Malachi wandered through the slippery elm grove. It was morel season, and the family had packed a picnic and gone mushrooming.

James-Cyrus bounced ten-month old Catherine in his arms. "Bouncy, bouncy, baby," he chanted. "Bouncy, bouncy girl." Catherine smiled and cooed, and grabbed at James-Cyrus's nose.

"That baby turns you into a pile of cornmeal mush," Cora said, reaching up and taking her granddaughter from James-Cyrus. She set the baby on the ground. Catherine looked around, then crawled off toward her mother.

Malachi wandered over and showed his harvest to Cora. "I did as you said, and took only half of what I found," he said. "There's still enough morels out there to feed every bear and skunk on this mountain and the next one, too." He glanced at his watch. "Shouldn't Hannah be here by now?"

"She had a delivery in town," James-Cyrus said. "She thought she'd be able to join us, but if there were any complications—"

"And there weren't, and here I am." A young woman of about thirty stepped out of the woods, her red hair blazing in the afternoon sunlight. "Am I too late for the party?"

James-Cyrus pulled her to him and kissed her deeply. "Hmm, you smell like baby powder and disinfectant. I like that in a woman."

Hannah laughed, then turned and hugged Malachi and Cora. "Thanks for inviting me today. I know this is a special day for you."

"Hannah! You made it!" Elizabeth joined them, the squirmy Catherine in her arms. She gave Hannah an awkward hug. "Kind of hard to hug someone with this wiggle monster in my arms."

"I love this wiggle monster." Hannah gave Catherine a kiss on the top of her head. "After all, I delivered her, didn't I?"

"And a lucky thing for James-Cyrus you did." Malachi reached out and took his daughter. "If you hadn't been Elizabeth's midwife, she couldn't have set you two up."

"Which reminds me, let me see it," Elizabeth demanded.

"See what?" Hannah's eyes gleamed with mischief.

"Come on, let me see!" Elizabeth grabbed Hannah's left hand, where a perfect heart-shaped diamond sparkled. Elizabeth hugged Hannah again, properly this time. "I'm so happy for you," she whispered.

"We're all happy," Cora agreed. "I'd begun to think this boy was never going to settle down." She poked James-Cyrus playfully.

"Just waiting for the right girl, Triple-G'ma," he said. The nickname had stuck, much to Cora's delight and amusement, and James-Cyrus rarely called her Cora anymore.

They feasted on a picnic of fried chicken, potato salad, and pickled okra. Cora had made sweet tea and lemonade, and Elizabeth had baked one of her fabulous cherry pies. Little Catherine fell asleep with a piece of okra clutched in her hand.

James-Cyrus smiled appreciatively at his beautiful wife-to-be, as she sat chatting with Elizabeth. He had thought love too dangerous, that a heart that loved was a heart asking to be broken. Cora's mother-love for Elizabeth and her determination to rescue her daughter from a tragic fate had changed his mind. Seeing the love shine in Malachi's eyes when he looked at Elizabeth had made him downright jealous. But then, he'd met Hannah, bright, funny, beautiful Hannah, who not only loved him fiercely, but loved his family as well, never questioning the bizarre story he told her of how they all came together through the magic of the fairy stones. Love might be dangerous, he thought, but it definitely is a risk worth taking.

"James-Cyrus, does Hannah understand what we're doing here today?" Cora began packing up the leftover food.

"I explained it to her," he answered. "We're returning the fairy stones to where you found them."

"The only thing I don't understand," Hannah cut in, "is why you waited until now to do it. If the Grandmother said the fairies wanted the stones back, why not return them right after Elizabeth and Malachi were rescued?"

"I thought about that," Cora said, digging around in the picnic basket as if looking for something. "But I thought it important that we wait for the baby to be born; that all the lives affected be here to give thanks when the stones are returned. Besides, I took them while I was hunting morels. I thought it fitting to return the stones when the morels returned. In the world of magic and fairies, timing can mean everything."

She pulled a small silk bag containing the fairy stones, a bag of cornmeal, and a trowel from the basket. "Ah, here they are. I was afraid for a moment I'd forgotten the very thing we came up here for."

"Should we wake her up?" Elizabeth asked her mother, gently rubbing her daughter's back.

"Bring her, but let her sleep for now," she said. "They'll understand."

They made their way over to an ancient slippery elm tree, the largest in the grove. There, they formed a circle, surrounding the tree. Cora shook a little cornmeal from the bag into her hand, then passed it around the circle, each person following her lead, Elizabeth putting a few grains in her sleeping daughter's hand.

Cora then began to speak.

"Oh guardians of this ancient grove, we thank you for the gift of your fairy stones, that saved three lives and set one free. We bring offerings of cornmeal, that you never hunger."

In unison, the group sprinkled the cornmeal on the ground.

Cora pointed to a spot beneath the tree, and James-Cyrus gently dug a small hole with the trowel. Cora then gently laid the three fairy stones in the hole and covered them with earth.

"What was torn asunder is now reunited. Now this grave wrong has been righted," she said. She rose to her feet.

They stood in silence for a few moments, listening to the wind in the trees and the call of a mockingbird in the distance.

"So mote it be," Hannah said.

"So mote it be," they all said in unison.

Epilogue

Thirteen-year old Catherine was a mountain girl at heart. Her grandmother had told her glorious tales of growing up on Hoffmann mountain, and now that she was gone, Catherine found herself spending more and more time wandering the trails and groves grandmother had loved so much.

It was a beautiful spring day, and even though her mother and Aunt Hannah were counting on her and her cousin Corrine to babysit her little brother William and Corrine's baby sister Eliza, keeping them in the house away from the hot cauldrons while they put up a year's worth of strawberry preserves, she couldn't bear the thought of being cooped up all day.

She stopped at the cemetery where Cora had been buried just weeks ago. "I miss you, Grandmother," she whispered, placing a bouquet of coral bells on the grave. They had been one of her grandmother's favorite flowers.

Leaving the cemetery, she ran up the trail to the slippery elm grove. Perhaps if she brought home a bag full of morels, her mother and aunt would forgive her for skipping out on the jam chores. Her cousin would certainly forgive her, for Corrine herself had more than once skipped out on babysitting duties, leaving Catherine to do double duty.

There were more mushrooms in the grove than she had ever seen before. Pulling her knife from her pocket, she began cutting stems, carefully taking no more than half the mushroom, as she had been taught.

The largest patch of morels was beneath the tallest, oldest tree in the grove. For reasons she never quite fully explained, her grandmother had never allowed her to harvest the mushrooms there, saying that patch of ground was too sacred. But there were so many, Catherine didn't see any harm.

She knelt down and was about to cut a stem when something caught her eye. Digging in the dirt, she pulled up a stone, about the size of a chestnut, in the perfect shape of a cross. She stood and brushed away the dirt. The stone was warm to the touch, not cool like she would have expected.

"Hello, what's this?" she said, cradling the stone, as the wind through the trees whispered, *"Believe what you see. Believe what you see…"*

MEET SMOKY TRUDEAU

Smoky Trudeau grew up on the flat plains of Illinois, but her happiest childhood memories are of the extended camping trips her family took each year to the mountains of Virginia, the eastern shore of Maryland, or—her favorite destination—the Great Smoky Mountains of Tennessee.

Graduated from North Central College in Naperville, Illinois, she jokes that it took her 17 years to complete her degree because she majored in everything except physics.

Her diverse interests led to a career as a freelance writer; her articles appeared in publications such as *Chicago Parent, Natural Health,* and *First for Women.* Her newspaper column, "Earth Beat," ran in several Illinois newspapers.

Smoky's short stories have appeared in *Potpourri* and *CALYX;* her collected short stories were published in 2003. Her story, *The Last Flight Home,* was nominated for the 2003 Pushcart Prize. She writes books reviews and the occasional article for *SageWoman* and *Pan Gaia* magazines.

Smoky works as a freelance editor and private writing coach, and has taught writing and creativity workshops at venues nationwide. She lives in Central Illinois with her daughter Robin (she also has an adult son, Steven), two dogs, two cats, a guinea pig, and a cantankerous geriatric cockatiel. When not writing, she enjoys jewelry making, sculpting goddess figures, and organic gardening.

Printed in the United States
119303LV00001B/118/P